Hearts at Grace Doorsteps

Hearts at Grace Doorsteps

Grove Hill Series
Book 1

Elle H. Raye

Hearts at Grace Doorsteps

Library of Congress Cataloging-in-Publication
Names: Raye, Elle, H., 1958-
Title: Shadows in Emma's Heart/Elle H. Raye, P-152
Description: East Texas, Christian fiction
Identifiers: LCCN: Library of Congress Control Number: 2023911769
Subjects: Fiction | Christian Fiction | Love Stories | Man-Woman
Classification: LCC | DDC LC record available at http://lccn.loc.gov/ 2023911769

ISBN: 9798223946168
Cover Art by Elle H. Raye

~ Dedication ~

To my Lord and Savior, Jesus, through Him, all things are possible.

~ Key Verse ~

For we are God's handiwork, created in Christ Jesus to do good works, which God prepared in advance for us to do.

Ephesians: 2:10

~ Chapter One ~

Jeanne Adams skidded to a stop on her sister's back porch. The glorious sight greeting her took her breath away, and she gently patted her heart. "Oh, my." Like vapors floating off a cup of coffee, Jeanne's breath curled out when giggles spilled from her lips. "Snow, snow, snow!" The sweet memory of her joyous tenth birthday flashed when her father gifted her a new puppy. Happiness trilled through her heart then, as it did now, and she clapped. This was her first experience with the white fluffy stuff covering every inch of her sister's backyard in the Texas panhandle.

The brisk, cool air filled her lungs, and she marveled at the charming display. "Lord, it's so beautiful. Thank You."

Wonderment and imagination flooded her senses when she studied the source that produced such a stunning display. She pondered if the fluffy clouds held additional flakes and if more would sprinkle down. Her gloved hand stretched into the sky, hoping to touch even one of the marvelous white and gray floaters, but that was impossible, and she knew that, but it didn't mean she couldn't try.

Overnight, four inches of snow settled across the small town of Grove Hill, and Jeanne planned on reveling in the white stuff. The neighborhood and community were not like what she had grown up in, but the warmth of love permeated her soul during the summer visits with her sister and family. Upon her insistence, her parents allowed this extra break before the holiday season began.

A gust of frigid wind whipped through her coat, and an icy shiver raced over Jeanne's body. When she left Hopewell two days ago, she hadn't checked the forecast and never imagined the temperatures would dip this low since arriving. In her nineteen years, never before had it got this cold in her hometown in far East Texas prior to the holidays or snowed—perhaps she'd been mistaken about the cold but not the snow. She pulled the borrowed white faux fur scarf tighter around her neck. Eyeing every inch of the yard for the best space to create her art was a task. *Which is my perfect area?* Marie, her niece, shared that the first snow was the best when making an angel.

Jeanne closed her eyes, taking in the stillness of the blanketed area, and considered that nothing else was on the planet but her. Then she recalled a question that was asked back in sixth grade when a meteorologist visited. The student's question sprang forward. "I vacationed in Colorado last winter, and it snowed. Why is it so quiet after it snowed?" The man's answer boggled her mind both then and now. "Snow absorbs sixty percent of the surrounding sound." She tilted her head and listened. The man was right.

While Jeanne played with her niece and nephew yesterday, she'd noted all the yard's pitfalls, flowerbeds, left-out water hoses, lawn equipment, and the children's forgotten toys. Her eyes fluttered open, and this morning's second greeting was just as marvelous as the first. With the perfect spot in sight, Jeanne stepped from beneath the porch canopy and carefully inched along the snow-filled sidewalk.

Ready, she spread both arms wide and fell backward into the fluffy powder. The coldness enveloped her body, soft as she'd imagined it should've been, and she giggled. *I'm lying on one of Heaven's clouds.* What must the neighbors think of her giggling? If they saw her joy, she was assured they'd understand. Then she flapped her arms and legs until satisfied with her efforts.

A mixture of excitement and dismay gave her pause when she could not comprehend how to get out of her perfect creation without wrecking it and making the art unrecognizable. If she rolled over on her side, it would be too fat and perhaps resemble a cow—that wouldn't do. Coming up with a quick plan, she drew her knees together, pushed with her hands, and stood. After tiptoeing to the edge, she stepped onto the pavement. Her foot smoothed a couple of divots. A wide-mile smile stretched across her lips, and her hand covered her heart as she admired the angel.

The back screen door jetted open, and little feet scampered across the porch. Marie and Brice, her sister's three- and four-year-olds, scurried into the yard as if a horde of bees was chasing them. The art lay in ruin, trampled into a sad array of angel parts and small shoe prints.

Jeanne's shoulders slumped. She could not fault the children for destroying the figure. They were eager to play, but she wished she could have enjoyed the angel a little longer than thirty seconds. *I can always make another one.*

The screen door clicked shut, and Renee's warm breath billowed out, reminding Jeanne of a dragon she had read about in a child's storybook years earlier. "You children play nice. I'll have hot chocolate ready when you come back inside." She smoothed back a long strand of dark hair that slipped out of the clip. "Jeanne, did you make your snow angel yet?"

Throughout the years, Jeanne hadn't noticed that everyone in the family had much darker hair and features than hers. Her appearance was altogether different, with blonde hair. As she matured, she often compared the other siblings to herself and found no similarities. She reasoned that she had not grown into her looks yet like the rest of the family.

Jeanne pointed at the leavings—children's shoe impressions trailing across the once perfect snow angel.

Renee's smile vanished, and she grimaced. "Oh, no. It's ruined."

"I'll make another one after the kiddos go inside. Until then, I'll take you up on some of that hot chocolate." Rubbing her gloves together, anticipating the delectable drink to stave off the chill in her bones.

Renee hooked her arm into Jeanne's. "Good, we can have a long talk while the kiddos play."

Has Renee sensed my confusion and unhappiness?

Jeanne's current lifestyle back home kept her on her knees each morning and again most nights. She held the purpose of the extra visit near her heart, not quite able to share the reason with folks here or at home. Sometimes thoughts of running away crossed her mind with the constant strict rules that pummeled her spirit, but she dismissed them and believed the Lord's peaceful refuge would guide her. She was unaware if her older siblings had aversions to these limitations—they seemed more restricting now than when the house was full of children. If so, they never confided in her.

Generations of Adams' attended the same denominational church adhering to the rules that flowed into the family structure. A modern world surrounded her, and these statutes needed changing—or so she often told herself. But that was out of the question, at least while still living in her father's house. Not once had she mistrusted her upbringing, but then she read a Bible passage that didn't match what her parents taught. Now she questioned everything that she heard. Did she misunderstand the verse and her parents, or was she being directed toward a different life plan than the one she'd envisioned?

The dutiful life at home required all to marry within their faith, and they could not develop friendships beyond the family unit or the church community. Since graduating high school five months ago, her father considered her a woman of marrying age. With her new status as a woman, she often felt trapped when men asked her on dates, but none were interesting, and she definitely was not searching for a husband right now. Guys her own age were silly and too immature.

Jeanne sensed the isolation, being the last child at home who had not settled into a loving family life like her four older brothers and sister. She missed the daily interaction with her siblings, and loneliness crept in more since growing up in a large household. Or had the visits with Renee and her husband put into play a disagreeable temperament? One day she'll take that step toward her dream of attending college to become a life coach to counsel tweens and young adult women to become stronger Christians and to rid the hurt inflicted by others. For the last two years, she felt and heard the Lord's small, still voice during her daily devotional time with Him to help girls. But how?

Renee and Winston Bryson attended the same denomination she did. Still, their members embraced the community, and she often heard this very thing from her sister but had yet to witness their neighborly love during her short summer visits. She welcomed the change and opportunities God would place before her on this trip.

Steam swirled upward from a batch of tummy-warming hot chocolate. With one last stir, Renee pulled the pan off the stove, filled two cups, and sprinkled the top with mini marshmallows. "Here you go, sis. It's still hot, so be careful."

Jeanne cocked her head, then her nose scrunched. Renee recognized the signal to back off from trying to mother her little sister and offered her a sweet smile. At ten years older than Jeanne, she looked after her on many occasions when she was a child, but they had limited time together the last five years since she married and moved to Grove Hill. Renee missed their daily interactions and hoped this visit would be good for both.

Instead of deepening their sisterhood bond, she sensed their relationship growing apart.

"Thanks." Jeanne cupped her hands around the mug, warming her fingers.

Renee claimed the kitchen chair across from her sister. "When you were my kiddo's age, you loved tiny marshmallows, and you'd cry every time they'd melt. Do you remember?" She brought the cup to her nose and took a good whiff. *Mmm, chocolate.* Cautiously she sipped, enjoying the sweet liquid.

Jeanne giggled. "I still want to when they melt, but I promise not to cry today. I didn't know anyone noticed."

Renee had indeed noticed a lot about her sister's summer visits over the years. How much she'd matured into a beautiful woman, and her self-confidence had grown since she graduated high school months ago. "I did. So, what's on your mind, sis?"

Jeanne gazed at the little white floaters like they had done when she was little, vanishing into the hot chocolate. "Nothing...nothing at all."

"I've known you for nineteen years and can always recognize when you're upset. Come on, tell me, and we'll pray about it together. The Lord is with you to guide you."

"Ree, I've already done that for some time now, but—?" She nibbled on her bottom lip and refused to look her in the eye.

Renee patted her hand. "Since your arrival two days ago, you've been praying in the middle of the night. So what is it? What has you so troubled?" *She wants to talk, but how long before she confides in me? I'll need to give her space. I pray that it's not a boy or even worse. Has she sinned? Guide my words. I don't want to offend her integrity.*

The younger woman finally lifted her chin and met Renee's gaze. "Sorry about waking you. Did I disturb Winston too, or did you tell—" She swallowed hard. Tears were on the verge of spilling from her blue eyes. Jeanne sniffed, smoothed a fallen blonde strand, and squared her shoulders. "I'm fine. Really, Ree."

Renee gently squeezed her little sister's hand. "Whenever you're ready to talk, I'm here. My husband doesn't need to know anything between us. Our sisterhood bond takes precedence." Renee pinned Jeanne with a stare. "The only concern in my heart is...did you sin? I mean—" Renee couldn't finish that sentence, but she must know how to intercede with a prayer to protect her sister.

Jeanne shook her head. "No, no. Never would I do such a thing. We've talked about that precious gift that'll be saved for my wedding night. Trust me, sis...." Again, she swallowed back tears. "It kinda looks like Winston has taken his mother's passing hard. How is he? Weren't they close?"

Renee blew across the cup and then smiled. "Thanks for that assurance." *All right, sis, whenever you're ready to talk.* "Even though the doctors said his mother's cancer was in remission, her sudden death took all of us by surprise. Her heart couldn't withstand the chemo and radiation treatments. Winston had hoped his brother would make it back for her service. Some days my husband struggles. I try to lift some of the burden, but nothing I've tried has worked. He prays daily that Roland isn't ill or worse, dead somewhere with a 'John Doe' tag attached to his toe."

"How are you managing the extra funeral expenses? I have a few dollars saved up from babysitting, chores for the elderly, and graduation money. I'll be happy to help in any way I can."

The air in Renee's lungs seemed to vanish as memories crowded in. Shortly after her and Winston's wedding, they moved to Grove Hill to help with his father's terminal illness and take over the business. A year after the older man's death, and with limited funds, the couple stayed on to run the family business and care for his mother. His eighteen-year-old brother, Roland, left home the day after their father died—he didn't attend the funeral, nor his mother's. Nearly a year later, he wrote saying he had joined the army. Another year passed, and another letter arrived, saying he was in Federal prison for six months after striking an officer and would be dishonorably discharged. Roland's letter gave a brief narrative of why he landed in prison. His last known address was in California. Since Winston's mother's passing, he tried to contact him but received no response. They assumed Roland either didn't get the message or didn't care, but they fretted about the alternative.

"You're too young to worry so much. We have a plan in place for the finances, but thanks for the offer." Renee took a playbook from Jeanne about changing the subject so quickly and pulled her daily planner from the middle of the table, where she kept it handy to manage her busy schedule. She didn't want to discuss the burden of finances with her sister—it wasn't her problem, but it was kind of her to offer her assistance. As she flipped through the pages, most days were filled with some sort of activity, whether at the church, Winston's job, or with the children.

She wanted to find a little wiggle room to spend more time alone with her sister, but nothing looked promising. The week already looked full. Except. *Hmm.* She unfolded a brochure and eyed the page, hoping Jeanne would get curious enough to ask, but she didn't.

So she slid the paper in front of Jeanne. "It'd be nice if you'd join me at the church's community mission. We're helping some locals by handing out blankets, jackets, and groceries. Most of these folks don't have heat in their homes, or the utilities went unpaid, so they were turned off. Afterward, I'm headed next door to help feed those who sheltered from the below-freezing temperatures last night. My church sheltered the homeless men, and the women slept at another church, but anyone is welcome to come in for a meal."

Jeanne cupped the warm mug and leaned in to read the flyer. “I’ll think about it. When is it?”

“Tomorrow. Today they are only handing out cold sandwiches and hot coffee. We can spend some quality time together helping those who need it in a big way. Usually, with this much snowfall, it stays on the ground for days because of the steady low temperatures. So don’t worry about the destroyed snow angel. You can make a new one soon.”

A burst of giggles spilled from Jeanne’s lips. “Oops, I almost forgot about my redo. You said your church, right?”

“Yes, dear. Our church. The same one you attend with us on your summer visits. Grace Chapel Church embraced us when we needed it most. The pastor and his wife truly have servants’ hearts. Winston and I love them and the community. When we decided to transfer our membership, it was easy. This church isn’t the same one Winston grew up in, and it’s sort of different. We needed a change and welcomed it. What’s wrong?”

“You spoke about the church ministries before during my summer visits but mentioned nothing beyond that or your involvement. You know my home church doesn’t respond to the community’s needs.”

Renee shrugged. “Your visits in the summers...well, I don’t volunteer, so we’d have more time together. Our congregation does a lot of community services, and we have friends outside the church."

Her little sister's eyes widened. "Really? If that's the case, I'll be glad to go. I've always wanted to see how the rest of the world lives." Her brow furrowed. "I didn't mean that the way it sounded, but you know what I'm trying to say, sis?"

Renee's previous church in Hopewell loved and worshipped God, but they only helped those in their inner circle. Community work was never a part of things, and the way her sister replied, nothing had changed. "Yes, I do. When I help those who seek something more than clothes or natural food. I know their souls are hungry, and they're seeking to be fed. I find it very fulfilling to serve others, and so does Winston. These folks are just like us...I mean, they have problems and hardships too. Some have fallen on hard times and need a helping hand occasionally.

"Not all are Christians, so it's up to us to show them a Jesus who is kind and willing to help when needed. I never understood why our hometown church never offered to help others. They wanted other churches in the community to oversee that part of serving. When Winston and I began attending this church, we quickly discovered that we don't feel that way."

"Have you told our parents about your family's activity in the new church?"

"Yes. Winston backed me, letting them know this was our decision. They can't live our lives, and we can't live theirs."

"Wow. You stood up to Dad."

"We did." Renee patted Jeanne's hand. "It's all good. They haven't disowned us, at least not yet. Finish your hot chocolate, and I'll bring in the kiddos so you can make a new snow angel."

~ Chapter Two ~

Jeanne rubbed away sleep with the heels of her palms, yawned, and stretched. Her bed at home was a lot softer, but she didn't mind one bit—not today. "Thank You, Lord, for this day and for letting me go with Renee to help the community with their needs. Please show me where I'm most needed. Let others see Your light through me." She stood and raised both arms toward the ceiling. A few kinks needed a little help, and she was ready to start her morning chores before heading to the church. She stripped the sheets off her bed.

When she arrived in Grove Hill, she and Renee had agreed upon which tasks were hers. Back in Hopewell, Jeanne always rose early to do her household chores and then go to school. Even here, she didn't deviate from those morning habits. Dressed, she stood and seated her feet in her boots.

Curiosity nipped at Jeanne. Had the snow in the backyard melted? She lifted a slat in the blinds and peeked outside—no new snow, but the yard still lay under plenty to play in later. She could not see the angel she had made yesterday from her window. Joy still trilled within from creating the second snow angel. She giggled to herself at the thought of seeing the art. *They say practice makes perfect, and I guess it must be true. The second snow angel I made yesterday is even more beautiful than the first one. I'll check it when I get to the dining room.*

A gentle tap on her door preceded Renee's whisper. "Are you up, Jeanne?"

"Ready when you are." She grabbed the bundle of sheets, the borrowed jacket, and the scarf and greeted her sister with a huge smile. "I've been up for an hour."

Renee's laugh echoed down the hallway, and she quickly clamped a hand over her mouth. "Oops, I don't want to wake the house. Let's go. I packed a thermos of coffee to take along. The church's brew is a little strong for my taste. You can start the laundry when we get back this afternoon."

"Perfect." With her free hand, Jeanne eased the bedroom door shut.

Even though the family were deep sleepers, the women moved quietly and quickly down the hallway.

Jeanne's boot toe banged against a table leg in the kitchen while trying to get a glance out the window to the backyard. "Oh, dear." She halted, tilted her head, and listened. Silence filled the house. Glad her snow angel was still intact. "Are Winston and the kids joining us today?"

Renee packed cups, snacks, and a thermos in a large sunflower tote. Jeanne suspected her sister had sewn the bag. Growing up, she'd always helped their mother make clothes for the family. Mom called her eldest daughter a "born seamstress." She boasted that from the time Renee had turned seven, her sewing gift flourished—with or without a pattern handy.

"They will join us later at the center where we'll feed the homeless." Renee smiled. "Would you like to drive?" She dangled a set of keys on one finger.

Jeanne had hoped she'd have time to practice her driving skills during her visit. "Really? I sure do."

"The roads are a little slippery, so take it easy. Has Dad let you get a car?"

"Thanks, sis. No, I'll tell you all about that argument shortly."

The women carried the bags and other provisions to the car and packed them into the trunk. Settled behind the wheel, Jeanne started the engine, pulled out of the driveway, and maneuvered through the streets as Renee directed her to the center.

Jeanne considered the task a *new adventure*, a burst of love and joy in the new day. Was this what she sought? Was that nudge in her spirit leading her to this district and church? Her morning prayer had included a promise that she'd accept whatever was gifted to her on this day with gratitude—whether physical or spiritual.

She gripped the wheel tighter. “Dad won’t let me drive much at home, and I can’t talk him into buying me a car.” A disconcerted breath puffed from her lips. “He keeps saying my husband will buy me a vehicle when I marry.” She glanced at her passenger. “Yesterday, you said this church doesn’t believe in marrying strictly inside the congregation?” Within her community, the pressure grew greater each season. And she planned on not helping it to evolve further.

“We welcome all non-members through our doors. If a couple is similarly matched, we embrace the relationship. The pastor requires them to go through counseling before the ceremony. Marriage is, after all, a lifetime commitment.” Renee smiled. “The union will be blessed who understands and keeps His covenant.”

Jeanne’s gaze remained on the road. “I like your church more and more. Sunday can’t get here fast enough so I can hear the message.” She angled the car into a snow-covered parking spot. At least, she hoped she wasn’t mistaken about the slot. The women retrieved the bags and stepped onto the hazardous walkway.

Renee clasped Jeanne’s hand. “Be careful, sis. It’s a little slippery. Looks like the men haven’t had time to shovel a path to the door.”

"I'm good. Don't worry about—oh!" Her right foot slid as she stepped onto the sidewalk, and her hand tightened on her sister's. "Catch me!"

Renee let the sunflower tote drop to the walkway. She reached for Jeanne's other hand…or any body part she could grasp to prevent a disaster. Suddenly, both women lay sprawled on their backs on the snow-covered grass, laughing.

A short young man appeared in front of the ladies. Renee's face paled. She covered her mouth to smother the giggles. "Morning, Pastor Eli."

"Are you ladies all right? Let me help you up, Sister Renee." He grabbed her hand, gave it a firm pull, and she landed on her feet. "You too, Ms."

"Pastor, do you remember my little sister, Jeanne Adams? She's visiting for a few weeks. Jeanne has shown interest in helping us today on our community project and even serving the meal."

"We can always use more helping hands. Good to meet you again, Sister Jeanne. Take hold, and we'll get you out of the snow."

Renee grabbed her sister's arm. "Sis, your arm is bleeding."

A red stain soaked through the sleeve of Jeanne's blue jacket. She glanced around the area and pointed out the guilty culprit to the pastor. A broken bottle poked its long neck through the snow.

"I'll have someone take care of that. Let's get you inside and check out the damage."

After Renee cleansed and bandaged the minor cut on Jeanne's forearm, the women began sorting blankets of all sizes, colors, and patterns. Lining the wall, large bins of coats and sweaters waited to be organized and hung on hangers so folks could select according to size what they needed.

Lots of women and men showed up to help with the tasks. Renee waved over a lady walking through the door. A blonde a few years younger than Jeanne approached them. "Jeanne, this is Madison Vanguard. She lives out in the country. Madison, this is my little sister, Jeanne Adams. She's visiting from Hopewell."

The women shook hands. Jeanne admired the woman's blonde hair gracefully dripping over her shoulders. Her deep blue eyes seemed to smile to be here. "Good to meet you. Do you also go to my sister's church?"

Madison shook her head. "I'm happy to meet you. No. I attend a different church not far from my house. You're welcome to join me and my family for services anytime."

Renee stretched her sight toward the door and touched Madison's arm. "Is Jimmy John and Mariah with you today?"

"Jimmy John had to work, and Mariah is sick with a stomach bug. But they promised they'll be here next time. Jeanne, I've known both of my friends since the fourth grade. We kinda hang out together doing things like this. I hope you meet them and join us for lunch or some of our social adventures before your visit ends."

"Sure. I'd like that very much. Just say when."

Renee touched Madison's arm. "How are you doing after...well, that bad experience?"

Madison heaved a sigh. "Fine, I guess. My heart is a little shattered after someone I thought was a friend, but her only motive was to trick Joseph into getting back with his ex-girlfriend. Hannah has never apologized for the mess she created. She said some awful things that weren't true. But I forgave them both and went on with my life." Madison looked at Jeanne. "I have very few friends—it's hard to trust now. Jeanne, I sense your heart." Her face lit up, and her smile returned.

Renee touched Madison's arm. "I'm sorry about such a thing happening to you, but yes, you can trust my sister. Thanks for sharing. I know how hard it is when someone deceives you. I'm glad you forgave them."

"I won't be friends with them—can't give them the chance to hurt me again. Thanks, Renee, and you too, Jeanne, for listening. We better get to work, so these folks can stay warm."

Someone called Madison's name from across the room. "See you guys later. I'm looking forward to getting to know you better, Jeanne." She waved, spun on her heels, and headed toward the man who beckoned her.

"Ree, I thought this was just for your church parishioners to work?"

"We welcome all to help. There are no denominations in the Lord's eyes. Mankind put that separation of God's children in place, and we ignore that everyone has a right to worship Him. We are all His children but don't act like it."

Jeanne blinked. "You're right. I hadn't seen it like that before. I'm glad Madison hasn't harbored bitterness against those who sought to use her."

"Me too. She has a good heart. Like yours, sis."

As planned, the volunteers finished before the doors opened to the public. Anyone could take whatever they required. Amazed, Jeanne's gaze took in the extensive line of people outside the entrance.

Her emotions spun in all directions. Joy and gladness that she could help, but also intense sadness at the sheer number of downtrodden people needing assistance. And these were residents. Were there this many in Hopewell who could use the same kind of aid? Why hadn't she noticed this before now? Had she been brought here for this very thing—to open her eyes—show her the circumstances, and strengthen her faith? Whatever the reason Jeanne felt the urging to hop a bus to Grove Hill, He was in control, and she would let Him lead.

A tired-eyed woman stood in line with three small children. Jeanne surmised that the youngsters were three to six years old. The two boys kept the mother on her toes. They'd punch each other's arms, burst into gales of laughter, and run in circles around their mother. More than once, she grabbed the little rapscallions by their shirt collars and whispered something in their ears. They'd settle for a minute but not for long. Occasionally, disaster was narrowly diverted when their rowdiness nearly knocked down other folks in line. Finally, the frustrated mom led the little girl to a row of chairs against the wall and ordered the child to sit there until her return.

Jeanne's heart pinched when tears spilled down the little blond-haired girl's cheeks—she had done nothing to warrant being disciplined. Perhaps the mother saw that her daughter might get injured by the brothers rowdiness. Dare she interfere with the parent's instructions or even offer a kind word to the girl, who was obviously hurt by her mother's words? Jeanne dropped the blanket onto a folded pile and strolled across the room. She sat beside the child and smiled. "Hi, my name is Jeanne. What's yours?"

The child sniffed loudly and wiped her hand across her nose. "Angel."

"My goodness, just like the angels in the Bible. How special to be named after one of God's creations. They watch over us, you know."

The child's eyes brightened, and a smile lifted on her lips. "Really?"

Jeanne focused her utter attention on the little one, letting the rest of the room's activities fall to the wayside. "Really. The Lord has special assignments for His angels. He has a mighty warrior archangel called Michael and a messenger angel called Gabriel. They do all kinds of things for God. So, what do you think?"

Angel's eyes had rounded on every word Jeanne spoke about angels. "Oh, my goodness." Tiny hands cupped her rosy cheeks.

Three pairs of feet stepped in front of Jeanne and Angel, ranging in size from kids to an adult. Angel's mother and brothers stood with their arms full of blankets and winter attire. The mother stared at Jeanne, then her gaze went to the child. "Time to go, Angel."

The little girl leaped off the chair. As one of her brothers led the child, she smiled broadly and waved at Jeanne.

Thank You, Jesus, for letting me give a moment of joy to one of Your children. Is this the reason I'm here today?

About an hour before midday, Renee rolled down her sleeves and smiled at her sister. "Grab your coat, sis, and we'll head to the shelter's kitchen to feed these folks a hot meal."

Aiding the locals made her feel useful and filled her soul with more love than she thought possible. Jeanne smiled when a verse from Matthew came to mind. "For I was hungry, and you gave me something to eat, I was thirsty, and you gave me something to drink, I was a stranger, and you invited me in."

When the women walked next door to the homeless shelter to feed men and women, Jeanne didn't think the day could get any better. But it did.

Roland Bryson wrestled with the decision to accept the pastor's offer and stay the night at Grove Hill's shelter. But with very few choices available to him, he must. His best-laid plan to arrive in his hometown before the first winter snowfall fell apart when overnight temperatures dipped below freezing and snow blanketed the region. With his aching body spent from an arduous trip, he longed for quiet, undisturbed, *refreshing* sleep that would clear away the fogginess in his head. In a shelter, none of those conditions were likely.

He stopped at the entrance and stomped off snow from his boots, not wanting to track inside. The room's capacity threshold must be pushing the limit. A crowd of men milled around as they claimed their cots. He sighed. *It's better than leaning against a dirty wall in the wet and freezing snow.* This long, grueling trip home provided him ample, though not always comfortable, time to reflect on his future and to pour his heart out to the Lord. The fellowship he had as a youth wasn't the same. Had he matured to a new level in their relationship?

Settled on a cot, Roland closed his eyes for the first time in days. Then, as he'd predicted, heavy snoring filled the combination shelter and food serving line room. To drown out the incisive noise, he smothered his head with the pillow but remained awake. The only bright spot left in his heart was anticipation—he couldn't wait to see his family—well, what remained of it after cancer took his dad five years ago, and then heart disease claimed his mother just last month, according to the message from his brother. He attended neither funeral.

Roland slept only a few hours between his roiling thoughts, the snoring, and dawn. He rolled up to a seated position, stretched, and glanced beneath the cot. His pack still lay where he had left it last night. After folding the blanket, he grabbed the pillow and placed both in a bin that held all the bedding for the cots.

Back at his designated space, he pulled his backpack from underneath the narrow cot and made sure his few belongings weren't disturbed. The zipper snarled on an envelope—and of course, the contents came to mind. His brother's written words sent a skittle along his spine. They were the reason no rush existed in getting to Grove Hill. By the time the mail had caught up with him, his mother's burial lay three weeks in the past. Would his family forgive him for running away years earlier? Would the daily guilt that besieged him ever go away?

Regardless of what happened, he'd promised himself never to leave the family or community again and prayed Winston's sincere letter was from love. His actions before and after his military career had to be faced, along with the shame—he saw them all every day when he looked at his own face in a mirror. His life needed prioritization, with the first to be God, his family, and a job. But how was he to conduct this latter feat? At his military sentencing trial, the judge told him that his army service record would follow him whenever and wherever he tried to seek employment. He ran his fingers through long, dirty, matted dark hair and planted his worn ball cap on top.

A firm hand latched onto his shoulder, and Roland spun on his heels. In a ready stance, his military training and a keen awareness of street living took over.

Pastor Eli stepped back and stared wide-eyed. "Sorry. I thought you heard me approach."

His shoulders relaxed, and he stuffed his fists into his jeans pockets. "Think nothing of it."

"The kitchen needs a headcount for lunch. Can you stay? We'll be happy if you will."

How could he not remain? "Um." *A hot meal wouldn't hurt*. "Sure. I'll stay."

"Afterward, a man is coming to offer haircuts and shaves at no charge." Pastor Eli cocked his head, and his eyes narrowed. "Son, do I know you? Are you from around here?"

Roland dipped his chin and looked away. "Too many years ago. I just got into town last night. My timing is a little off with the bad weather, but that's how it goes."

"Well, you're welcome to eat, get a haircut, and shave if you like." The pastor sighed. "We're not supposed to ask names, but have you ever visited Grace Chapel Church—"

"Pastor." A man cried out from across the room.

Pastor Eli gestured to the man. "Sorry, gotta go. We'll talk later."

Yep, pastor, you know me. You were several years ahead of me in school. I have all these doubts rambling around in my head. But I want my identity concealed for now. I'll depend on my military training until I'm accepted back into the community and my family. If Winston and Renee won't...Jesus, You're in charge, and whatever the outcome, I'm staying.

He busied himself helping the volunteers put up cots and setting out tables for the luncheon. He glanced in the pastor's direction occasionally and caught him studying him, but he kept his ball cap pulled down enough to hide his eyes—they had always given him away. No one in this community had blue-violet-colored eyes like his. Thanks to his eyes, the girls at school had flocked around him, but now they were a recognizable feature he could only hide for moments at a time.

After setting out the last table, he spotted a corner away from others where he could watch the front door. Living on the streets, he had learned never to trust anyone and to always keep his back against the wall. Experiences called for such actions on his part. On his first night on the streets, a man attacked him and stole his coat. Since then, he'd seen so many people with problems—drug addicts, victims of rape, and abused as the devil's hand definitely played against the destitute, most of whom had no means of defense, either spiritual or physical.

The aroma of food wafted into the room, and Roland pushed his cap up. His rumbling stomach made it clear he needed a meal.

Two young women entered and strolled across the room toward the kitchen. Were his eyes deceiving him? *Is that Renee and Jeanne? Oh...can I clean up enough to be accepted back? Please, don't let them recognize me...not right now, not looking like this.*

Blending in with the other folks outside was easy, but Roland's efforts were for naught in the center. A guilty twinge rippled through his gut. He slid the tattered bill of his cap further over his eyes and shifted his chair away from the others.

He glanced at his backpack. Stitched across the flap, "Bryson" flashed like a neon sign. *Surely that'll give me away.* He pivoted the bland-green pack, tucked it beneath the table, and settled a leg atop. He didn't want any family to come over, so he kept one eye on his sister-in-law and her sister and one on the door.

~ Chapter Three ~

Jeanne gathered her long blonde tresses and wrapped them atop her head in a messy bun—it would not do if hair got into anyone's food. After plucking two aprons off the rack, she joined Renee as the man in charge gave a short tutorial on each one's duties.

Renee was assigned to the potato salad station, and Jeanne distributed yeast rolls and homemade cornbread beside her sister. She breathed a silent prayer of thanks that those in charge of the kitchen didn't expect her abilities to be more on her first day. Never had she been one who stayed in the house to help her mother prepare meals. She preferred being on the Internet trying to figure out how she could manage to get into college without her parent's funds. Her lifelong dream was to help young women and tweens navigate life with God's influence. Most were broken, or injured by men, one way or another. So her cooking skills were minimal at best.

During the school year, she'd volunteer for the after-school programs to aid the girls in the lower grades with homework. Her parents didn't mind her activities, and she felt pressured to find a boyfriend after graduation. Actually, she wasn't interested, but the guys around her were too goofy. Besides, she longed to hone her skills in counseling the young. Jeanne had run across her heart's desire when she was a sophomore, and the school's counselor asked her to assist during the after-school programs. Jeanne saw firsthand how these young people lived in the community outside her own church's providence. Her heart broke. And ever since, she'd volunteered as much as possible of her time and efforts to help the counselor.

Needy men snaked around the walls. An outside line began at the door of mostly women, with a few men dotted here and there in between. The hopeless expressions across faces were disheartening. Jeanne lifted a smile, hoping it would offer some comfort, as they partook in a hot meal and the warmth of human kindness, even for a short while.

Her bones shivered as if she stood outside alongside these folks in the frigid weather. She glanced at the limited number of volunteers and saw she could not abandon her post to supply a carafe of hot coffee to stave off the bitter cold. Instead, she worked more quickly so they would get inside the center sooner.

Renee scooped up potato salad and reached across to place the portion on a man's plate, but she froze mid-motion. Jeanne patted her sister's shoulder. "What's wrong, sis?"

She shook her head. "Nothing, nothing at all."

The guy in front of her seated his cap further over his eyes and moved out of line.

"Ree, are you sure you're okay?"

Renee puffed out a heavy breath, dropped the utensil, and rushed through the kitchen's double doors.

Jeanne signaled a volunteer. "Please, take over for us. I'm sorry. I need to find out what's happening with my sister."

Not waiting for a response from Madison, she set off in a trot after Renee, dodging the kitchen staff all the while. On her first step out the door, her right foot slid on an icy patch, but she skidded to a stop.

Renee leaned with her back against a wall, hands on her knees. Her labored breath concerned Jeanne. Irrational thoughts frightened her, and she quickly rejected them—hoping her sister's reaction was not a physical ailment.

"What's wrong?" She stroked Renee's back.

"I think…I think Roland's here at the shelter—he's homeless. He's come home." Renee straightened and met Jeanne's concerned gaze.

"Really. That's great news. Where was he? Let's find him, sis." She tugged on her sister's sleeve.

"No…wait." Renee shook her head. "It'll be easier if he came home on his own. He took the first steps by being here, that's important. Something happened within the family before Winston and I were married. He never spoke of it, and I didn't push the subject. But sometimes, he's depressed, and I hear him whisper about being guilty when he is deep in prayer. I've prayed that all would be resolved with whatever occurred. Mention nothing to Winston about his brother. When he and the kids arrive, I'll tell him."

Jeanne nodded. "Sure. Which one was he? It's been about five years since I last saw him."

"He looks nothing like his pictures from high school or his military ones. His eyes are harsher but more mature. Something has changed him, and not for the better. Both Winston and Roland need our prayer."

The women gripped chilled hands and bowed their heads. Renee prayed softly. "Heavenly Father, You've brought Roland home safely. Thank You. Please fill his heart with love and rid it of any bitterness he might be harboring. Unite the brothers so they can forgive any wrong. Lord, You've gifted me with my family. What a blessing. We pray that we honor You as we serve Your children and hope they see You, not us, in our deeds. In Jesus' name, we pray. Amen."

"Amen." Jeanne drew her sister into a hug. "It'll be all right. God has this, and I'm certain He will answer our prayer. Let's get back inside. I'm freezing."

At arm's length, her sister smiled. "Okay. Oh, what time is it?"

"About a quarter after twelve. Why?"

"Winston said he'll finish at the shop and meet us around noon. They'll be here in a few minutes. How am I going to tell him about his brother?"

"You'll find a way. You always do, Ree."

Inside, Jeanne searched the room for the brother but saw no one remotely resembling the young man she met once at Winston and Renee's wedding. Had he left? Then she spotted a man in the far corner, alone. *Oh, no, Roland, what happened? Renee is right. You've matured, but...? Did the army cause this change? Why are you homeless? You have family, well—one brother, but Renee and the children are there. I'm sure whatever occurred can be ironed out and the relationship restored.*

Jeanne positioned herself behind the counter and shot up an additional quick, silent prayer for the restoration of brothers.

Renee smiled at an older man in the serving line and placed a scoop of potato salad on his plate. She kept a watchful eye on the front door, and her heart pounded each time it opened. As if on cue, her family entered. Renee shot up a silent prayer. *Give me Your strength and guidance as I tell Winston about his brother's return. I pray he'll accept Roland back into our family's fold. In Your Word, You say if we ask, we will receive, so I'm asking for our family to be whole again. Whatever Your will is, it'll be best.*

Little Brice wiggled his hand out of Winston's grip and headed straight for Jeanne, calling out her name. With the child in hand, Jeanne led him back to his father. The line had thinned, so Renee felt confident enough to step away for a few minutes after Jeanne's return.

Winston's handsome smile had always sent a flurry of love through her soul. Nothing had changed. She returned his smile with one of her own, hoping it still affected him in the same way it had before kids, the bills, and the responsibilities. "Hi, there. You guys arrived just in time. We're almost finished serving. We'll do clean-up shortly, and in about an hour, we can spend the afternoon together."

She bent and gathered her children into a hug. "How are my angels today?"

Both children smiled and replied in unison. "Okay, Momma."

Renee hugged them again, then stood and greeted Winston with a kiss on his cheek.

"Good, we didn't miss all the fun. Where do you want me?"

She'd fallen fast and hopelessly in love with Winston the instant they met. Daily, she thanked Jesus for bringing him to Hopewell that summer so he could apprentice at her neighbor's furniture shop. What a servant's heart he had.

"Sweetheart, I need to talk to you in private. Let's go into the kitchen for a minute."

Renee nodded at Jeanne, who kept sliding her glance toward them as she served the last few men in line.

An inquiring brow raised high on Winston's forehead. "All right." He sat the children at a table and knelt in front of them. "Stay here. Aunt Jeanne is just over there and will watch you guys. Mom and I will be right back. You guys can hug your aunt when we return, but you must stay here for now."

They nodded. Brice's little feet bounced up and down, ready to jump off the chair any moment. Winston patted his knee. "We won't be long." The child's foot calmed, and he nodded again.

Alone in the kitchen, Renee faced her husband, searching for a way to convey the secrecy, but a knot grew in her throat.

"Okay, what's so private you don't want Jeanne to know?"

Her hand gently laid on his, and she looked into his eyes. "She already knows. I hope you think this is good news." She steadied her breath, anticipated for the best, and dove right in. "Roland is here." Gauging his expression for any adverse reaction and she found none.

A broad smile spread across Winston's face as he peeked through the door's small window. "Where is he? Out there, in the dining room, or here in Grove Hill? Is he all right?"

Renee sighed. "Over there." She gave a sharp nod in the general direction. "He tried to hide from me by pulling his cap over his eyes, but I recognized those blue-velvet peepers when he came through the serving line. No one else around here has eyes like Roland's."

Her husband pushed on the door, but she gripped his arm. "Wait."

He didn't resist and spun back toward her. "What's wrong?"

Renee had to tell him what she'd seen in her brother-in-law. "He's not a volunteer...Winston, he's one of the homeless. He didn't speak to me nor I to him." She shook her head. "Something terrible must've happened on the streets that brought him home. Your mother's funeral was nearly a month ago…could that be it? You never told me why Roland left Grove Hill, and I understand if you don't want to talk about family issues."

"Homeless? I wish I knew why he left. Roland never confided in me. Maybe if he had, he wouldn't have left so abruptly. I, I sometimes blame myself for the cause of his leaving." Gently he gathered Renee's hands in his. "If you're willing to help me, we can get him back on track—if that's what he wants. How about drugs or alcohol?"

Renee smiled and tilted her head. "Of course, I want him home. We're family. His eyes were clear, and I didn't smell liquor, but I wasn't downwind."

As Winston peered through the porthole, she could tell her husband was working on a plan to bring his brother home. She tiptoed and settled her cheek against his as she, too, studied her brother-in-law through the glass. "I've got an idea. We'll send Brice over with a plate of food. You know our little boy can perceive the hearts of others. We'll watch from the serving line. I'm positive he'll be safe. Pastor Eli talked to Roland earlier and didn't seem alarmed by him in any way."

"If he came through the line once, will he question when Brice brings him a plate?"

"Maybe, but let's try, anyway. From what I saw that year after we were married and when you shared about his gentle ways as a youth, Roland will accept the kind gesture and won't think anything of it."

"Thank you, sweetheart. From his letter after what occurred in the service, my brother was ashamed, but he paid the price. I don't know the entire story, and I hope he will confide in me one day. I never have held that against him at all. Why he left home so quickly without a word, only a brief note scribbled on a paper napkin after Dad passed, is still a mystery to me." Winston blinked, clearly fighting tears.

Over the years, Renee saw her husband's guilt for what she figured was not his fault or anyone's, but she also sensed the discord within the family. She never asked about it, nor did Winston share the reason with her—she hoped all would be resolved in due time. "Roland will confide in you when he's ready. Until the reason is aired, stop blaming yourself."

"Something happened during the time I was in Hopewell. When Dad got ill and we moved here, I felt a strain on the family. But when he passed…." He shook his head. "Roland had withdrawn into himself and wouldn't speak to anyone, especially Mom."

Renee slung an arm across her husband's shoulder, hoping the gesture could ease his pain. "I'm sorry, sweetie. I was too busy being a new bride to take notice—I failed you and the family. Invite him home. I'm certain we can work through any problems." She lowered her gaze to the floor and hoped none of her actions back then were the reason for the division of the family.

He gently slid a finger along her jawline and lifted her chin to meet his gaze. "No, you didn't. You were, and still are, my rock and have been nothing short of supportive of my family and ours—thank you, darlin'. Of course, I want him home. He's my little brother. The question is, will he come? He may feel like the enormity of his situation would overwhelm the family."

She peeked through the window again. "I hope he doesn't talk himself out of staying. We gotta get back. The line is getting busy." She followed her husband through a set of double doors.

~ Chapter Four ~

While in line, Renee's expression conveyed she had recognized him. *She looked straight into my eyes. She's bound to know it's me. But I'm not ready yet, sis. Give me time ...please.*

A deluge of panic surged through Roland when Winston walked through the front door with his two children. Would his brother also recognize him? Delight surged across his soul that he had family nearby, but a simultaneous sadness settled in as he watched his brother with his niece and nephew. He had never seen them together. He pushed the cap's bill above his eyes to witness their interaction and what he'd missed over the years. The photos he'd taken off their social media page and transferred to his phone proved an enormous blessing. Those happy images helped him survive each day and night while he wandered the streets aimlessly, unsure of what he was searching for. He hadn't found it yet but trusted the Father directed the path he traversed.

They look happy. Can I have the same happiness in my life someday? Probably not, since I ran off like a thief in the night. Only You know I had a reason. I can't tell them what I know. It would break Winston's heart—and I'm not about to tarnish our parent's image, which you hold dear, brother.

Little Brice's hand wiggled out of his father's, then the child cut loose and ran toward the serving line. "Aunt Jeanne!" He disappeared between the legs of the people standing at the counter.

Winston pulled his daughter's hand closer, then his head bobbed and weaved, searching.

Roland gasped and jumped to his feet. *Is he okay? Winston, get that little man before he gets injured.*

As if on command, the line parted. A young lady appeared with his nephew in tow, leading the youngster to his dad. Her smile warmed Roland's heart. Something happened with his knees…they would not bend or cooperate as he gazed at the beautiful young woman. Her presence had been a mere shadow in his mind when he'd so desperately slinked away from the serving line and his sister-in-law.

The last time he saw Jeanne, she'd been an awkward teen, stumbling over the least of things on the aisle—even the rose petals the flower girls had sprinkled—while she tried to keep pace with the wedding march ahead of Renee. No longer a gawky teen, her gracefulness was breathtaking.

Her smile, her carriage…everything about Jeanne exuded the quiet confidence of a strong woman, and with her presence here today also witnessed her faith.

With both children in hand, Winston escorted them to a nearby table. He sat the kids in a chair, facing each other, then knelt between them. After a few words, the youngsters nodded and smiled. He wrapped his arms around them and planted kisses on their foreheads.

Although Roland had rested last night, his drained body still needed more nourishment. A second serving would give him energy, but he'd already gone through the line once and got a few portions on his plate, more than he had eaten the last three days. A loud and obnoxious growl came from his stomach, and he hoped those surrounding him didn't hear it. But if they did, they were fully aware of the sting of hunger pangs.

While he fought with himself regarding whether to get in line or stay put, his nephew approached with a plate of food. A chuckle softly released from Roland's lips as the child maneuvered around chairs and dodged people's legs, his tongue wiggling halfway out on one side of his mouth.

The youngster's steps slowed, the plate he carefully clutched tittered, and the boy stopped in front of Roland. He sucked in a breath when Brice thrust the meal toward him with a wide grin that spread cheek to cheek and displayed a gap where two front teeth once lived.

"Sir, here'th your lunch," the boy lisped through his unfamiliar missing teeth.

Roland nodded. "Thank you, little man." He hoped the boy would leave the plate and go, but he didn't.

A quizzical brow rose across the child's forehead as he searched Roland's face. "You look like the picthure of my Uncle Roland that'th on our mantle. He'th a tholdier. I'm gonna be a tholdier one day like him. He'th brave."

Roland glanced around the room to find his brother. *This kid recognizes me. They must have my photo in the family room.*

Winston stood with his daughter's hand in his and called out. "Brice."

"Gotta go. Bye, mithter."

His nephew ran toward his father, and Roland's gaze followed.

Then he saw her again. *Jeanne.* His heart skipped a beat. *Stop it—she's bound to be married or in some kind of relationship.*

The grit from his soiled clothes had flaked off with all his vaulting up and down, and the floor around his chair looked like a dirt bowl. Images of himself in the mirror when he'd visited the restroom, sent an unbearable deep knowing of what he had become in the last year. Homeless. Useless. A bum.

Roland's nephew darted off and jumped into his father's arms. Little Marie bounced on her toes and spread her arms wide, wanting her dad's attention. The sweet sight brought joy to Roland and sadness too.

Renee stood next to her husband, gently rubbing circles on his back. After two children and the tragedy in the family, his sister-in-law remained a strong, devoted woman. Her smile shone brightly. The same familiar one she'd used to comfort his dad during his illness. He recalled how she sang hymns daily until his dad took his final breath.

Roland glanced at Jeanne, whose similar smile had captivated his heart moments earlier. An adoring family scene played out as Roland watched, and a twinge rippled through him. He stood, heaved a heavy breath, slung his backpack over one shoulder, and strolled toward his family. Dare he approach them in the current state of his appearance—grizzly, dirty clothes and hair, and unkempt beard? But if not now, when? He took two steps forward, stopped, turned, and headed to the front door. He surprised even himself with his swift exit. He wasn't ready...not yet.

Outside, Roland ran across the street and darted into an alley. He rested against the dirty wall. *Safe.*

Moments earlier, when he'd approached the family, a vibrant flash of pain from his past filled his mind. All he saw was his father standing there. Winston and his dad had similar features, the same build, and dark brown eyes. During his dad's final days, his eyes grew darker and more menacing. Sometimes they haunted him in the middle of the night. He would wake in a cold sweat, shaken to the core of his being. "Why, Dad, why?" A sob-filled whisper spilled off his lips.

He watched the center's front door in case Winston or Renee followed. After a moment, he sighed, glad they hadn't. He squatted and buried his face in his hands. "I need Your strength. Can I tell Winston? Will this hurt in my heart ever heal? Jesus, You died for me, and I'm so grateful. Please stay with me. Guide me through this turbulent life I've chosen. I'd love to be with family, but how? I can't keep this secret from them much longer."

"Then don't."

Roland looked up with red, swollen eyes but could not recognize the man's features through his blurry vision. He rubbed away the tears with the heels of his palms and then focused on the man standing in front of him.

Pastor Eli held out his hand. "Let's talk, son."

He nodded, accepted the kind gesture, and stood. "I'm grateful He sent you."

Pastor Eli crossed his hands behind his back. "Want to walk for a while?"

"Sounds good." Roland pulled a hanky from his back pocket, ran it over his face, then hitched his backpack over one shoulder.

"So, tell me, what's going on?" The pastor held his gaze on the path while they strolled.

"It's a long story." Roland scuffed his boot toe on the snow-filled sidewalk.

"Take your time. I'm not going anywhere, son. I'm here to listen when you're ready, as is the Lord."

Roland's shoulders relaxed, Eli's solemn voice and temperament doing what they were meant to do—comfort the flock he shepherded. With the pastor being five years older than Roland, he surmised God had instructed this man well. "Pastor, you do know me. Before I left the community, I was a church member, and I think you graduated from high school the year I became a sophomore. I'm Roland Bryson, Winston's younger brother." He glanced at the man to see if he acknowledged their connection.

The pastor walked on, giving Roland only a nod of recognition.

He resumed. "Things went kinda sideways when Winston left to apprentice in Hopewell with a friend of my father's. I was around sixteen back then, a kid still. Dad said and did things—" He drew a deep breath. "Things that were not in his usual demeanor. We'd be in the shop working on a customer's project when he'd suddenly burst into a rage. He'd call me terrible names—I won't repeat the words. Then once...no, twice…he threw a hammer at my head. Luckily, it didn't make contact. Afterward, he cried and asked me to forgive him, and I did. But he continued to do those things again and again. Every day, I'd pray for

Dad's healing and deliverance from the illness that took control of his mind. Just before Winston married, Dad was diagnosed with a brain tumor." He paused, and a shuddered breath escaped. "Winston and Renee moved home, and I thought everything would return to normal after his surgery…but it didn't." Roland's sob-filled words halted.

Pastor Eli settled a hand on Roland's shoulder and gently squeezed. "You're doing fine, son."

They came upon the entrance to Grace Serenity Garden—a prayer garden adjacent to the church's grounds. Volunteers spent countless hours honing and chiseling Bible verses into the Texas Hill Country limestone walls for those who wished to take refuge within the garden.

"Shall we go in and have a seat?" Pastor Eli gestured toward the benches. After brushing snow off the seats, they lowered onto them.

Reliving that year sent spikes through Roland—today was the first time he had confided in anyone about the months of agony he endured at his father's hand. Roland released a heavy sigh and continued. "The name-calling stopped, but not for long. Dad started up again, and things got worse. When he healed from the surgery, he could work again in the furniture shop several days a week. I'd keep to myself, saying nothing when he was around." Recounting the experience caused the knots to return in his shoulders. "But then he took his grandfather's razor strap to my back—"

"Don't feel like you need to rush."

"Dad cried and asked forgiveness each time. Pastor, I did forgive him over and over again. I knew the man who'd been so abusive to me was not my father. The man who raised me didn't do things like that. Still, the scars remaining on my heart and across my back run deep. Then one day, Mom stood in the shop's doorway. She saw him, but she didn't stop his abuse. I never understood why." Tears trickled from Roland's eyes as he buried his face in trembling hands. He quickly shook his head and suppressed his emotions.

"I must've been a bad son. For the life of me, I don't have a clue what I did to warrant their abuse and rejection. They didn't do this to Winston. I did everything asked of me and then some—it wasn't good enough. I wasn't good enough to be the son they wanted or needed."

"You recognized the torture your father was in from the tumor. From what I've known about your father, I'm certain he was tormented with pain, even more with what he'd inflicted upon you and your mother. Your mother may have seen the abuse, and perhaps she also knew this wasn't her husband...the man she'd married and to whom she'd borne two sons. Did you speak to her about what happened?"

"No. We never talked about it. When she left the shop, tears streamed down her cheeks. Hopefully, she only saw the abuse one time."

"You may never know why she didn't stop your father. But be assured your prayers are heard. He loves His children, Roland. Direction, not intentions, determines your destination in life. We all look for satisfaction of one sort, but when you arrive where God intends for you to be, you'll find peace in your heart. You'll need to forgive yourself for your actions—I'm certain the family has. Talk to Winston, son. Come clean with your feelings and why you left the family. Your brother is an understanding and forgiving man. Look for that direction. And if you'd like, you're welcome to come home with me for a few days until you decide what's best."

Roland's brow furrowed. "Better check with your wife first. She may not want a stranger in the house." His arms spread wide. "I'm not the normal houseguest."

Pastor Eli chuckled. "We always keep a spare room available for anyone in need. You're more than welcome."

"Thanks, pastor. I'll take you up on the offer."

~ Chapter Five ~

Jeanne gasped and covered her mouth. What she'd witnessed floored her. She figured the brothers would reconcile since the entire family gathered in the center. Renee and Winston's hopeful countenance vanished in an instant when Roland walked out the door without so much as an acknowledgment of their presence. *Gone. What triggered such a reaction in the man to leave so fast? Please mend the divide between this family. Only You can.*

The serving line thinned enough for Jeanne to step away and join her sister and brother-in-law. She rounded the serving counter and slipped her arm over Renee's shoulders. "What just happened? Why did Roland leave so fast?"

Winston stared at the door and shrugged. "I haven't a clue." He gripped Renee's and Jeanne's hands. "We need to pray for my brother. I couldn't see his face well to see what spurred his action, but I know he needs uplifting."

With eyes closed and heads bowed, he cleared his sob-filled voice. “Heavenly Father, we praise Your holy name and are thankful for this chance to serve Your children at the center. Being Your hands is something You have blessed us with. You said that when two or more of Your children come together in agreement, You will be present. So, we are asking in total agreement that if it’s Your will, You’d please bring Roland home soon. We know You’ve directed him this far. Now would You continue to do so until he’s safely home—and we’ll never cease praying for him. Whatever he’s suffering through, please remove the burden and let him be assured we hold nothing against him—no blame, no bitterness, as You do the same with our repentance. If possible, would You guide someone to help or even offer a word of encouragement to my brother? We open our hearts and home to him. Surround him with Your hedge of protection. Again, Your will be done for him and us. In Jesus’ name. Amen.” At the center of the adult's circled prayer, two little voices softly said. “Amen.”

Jeanne released Winston’s hand and pulled Renee into a hug. “You guys take a short break. I’ll watch the kids.”

“Thanks.” Renee tugged on her husband’s sleeve. “Let’s take a stroll to the Garden for a minute.” She turned toward Jeanne. “We won’t take long. The sidewalks still have a couple of inches of snow on them.”

Winston nodded, followed his wife through the kitchen, and exited the back door.

Her brother-in-law's chest literally deflated when his brother walked out the door, and Jeanne knew he needed some time to recover from the harsh shock. Both did.

She knelt in front of Marie and Brice. "Your mom and dad needed a minute together, and they'll be back shortly. In the meantime, how about we play a word game?"

The two dark-headed children nodded. "We don't know how to play that game, Aunt Jeanne." Brice glanced at his sister as if she would back him up. And she did with a nod.

"I'll teach you guys, and it'll be fun. My teacher in first grade used to tell her class to put on our thinking caps." Jeanne cupped her hands and moved them over her head as if she were actually setting a cap on top. She giggled to herself as she recalled when she carried out this very act as a child. "You children do the same."

Little hands mimicked her actions by placing an invisible cap on their heads. "All right, children, look around the room and pick out one or two things you like, and then you tell me. I'll spell the word first, and then you try. Afterward, we'll use the words we spelled to make up a story. Does that sound like fun?" Every time Jeanne visited her family, she took delight in reading to the children at bedtime or whenever she got the opportunity. She always felt the more children read or being read to, immensely benefited them when they started school.

Smiles spread wide across the children's faces, and their gazes swept the room, searching for a particular object. When finished, they turned back to Jeanne.

"Brice, you're the oldest and have heard many more words and stories than Marie, so is it all right if she goes first?"

"Sure." He patted his sister's back. "Go ahead, Marie."

"Sweetie, what did you see?" Jeanne encouraged.

The little girl brought a finger to her cheek, tapped it a few times, and then smiled. "Chair."

"Okay, chair. Brice, can you spell the word chair?"

"No." His chin dipped, and he ran a sleeve across his nose. "Should I?"

"You will after we finish, so don't worry. I'll spell it first, and then you guys try."

Brice nodded. Marie followed his lead.

Slowly Jeanne spelled the word. "C-H-A-I-R. Marie, you try."

"C-A-I…um…R. Is that right, Aunt Jeanne?"

"Almost. Okay, your turn." She gave her nephew a smile and a supportive nod.

A deep line creased across the little boy's forehead. "C-H-A-I-R."

"Correct. Very good, Brice." She rewarded him with a kiss on his forehead. "Marie, did you hear which letter you missed in the word?"

"No." The little girl shook her head. Her bottom lip quivered, and her eyes filled with tears that threatened to spill over.

"Sweetheart, it's okay if we don't get things right the first time. Your brother Brice is older, so don't think you can't do what he does or even better, and we each learn differently. I'll spell it again for you, okay? Listen closely."

Marie stepped closer and slid her little hand into her aunt's. Jeanne wanted to giggle, but that might discourage or even hurt the child's feelings, and she would never do that to such a precious, innocent child. "C-H-A-I-R. Your turn."

Little Marie's grip tightened. "C-H-A, um, I-R." She stared at her aunt.

Jeanne smiled and rewarded her with a kiss on her forehead, just as she had with Brice. She definitely didn't want the children to compete at this early age. "Correct. Great job, both of you. I'm proud of you guys."

Suddenly, Renee and Winston hurried into the room like jackrabbits being chased by a coyote.

"Children, we'll finish our game later." Jeanne smiled, and the two little ones nodded.

Renee's scrambled words made no sense. Then she drew a calming breath and spoke clearer. "Jeanne, we just saw Roland getting into Pastor Eli's car. It looks like he's taking him home."

Confusion smothered Jeanne's thinking. "What does that mean? Does he need to talk to him or correct something he did?"

"Oh, I forgot, you're unaware that Pastor Eli and his wife often invite someone he trusts into their home as long as they want. This is so great."

"Is it?"

"Roland is staying in Grove Hill. With the pastor helping with his spiritual and physical needs, it won't be long before he's home with us. We just have to give him space. Our prayers have been answered and sent someone to do what we couldn't."

"We prayed for Roland to come home, not for him to stay with someone else. I don't understand, Ree."

"Yes, we did, but this is better. The situation is under control. He'll come home shortly, you'll see. Thank you, sis, for believing in prayer and helping us."

"You're welcome. I hadn't figured it'd be this fast. Winston, this quick action deserves our thanks for this swift blessing?"

Her brother-in-law's smile widened. "Roland is not home yet but has taken a step toward us. Let's bow our heads. You too, children."

With their heads bowed, they thanked the Lord for His utmost and swift attention.

Pastor Eli led Roland to a side door of his home. "We use this suite for guests since Cheryl's mother passed away—"

Roland could see the pain was still raw. "My condolences. How long has it been, Pastor?"

A tear rolled off the pastor's cheek. "January will be a year. Cheryl's parents had her late in life. Her father died of a heart attack when she was two, and her mother had dementia and died younger than most with the disease. She struggled with it over the years, and then when the medicine became less effective, she chose to stop all of it. Her last days were peaceful, and it was a blessing to Cheryl and me when she recalled my wife's childhood and sang hymns." He cleared the emotion from his throat. "Come on in and make yourself at home."

After unlocking the door, he pushed it open and dropped the key in Roland's hand. "Be sure to lock up when you go out. We might be a small community, but we still have those who wonder through the area that must steal for drugs or survival."

Roland was well aware of those types and encountered them far too often on the streets. He stopped short of stepping over the threshold and imagined his worn boots were glued to the stoop for some reason. "Are you sure this is okay with your wife? I mean…um…this was her mother's space."

Pastor Eli nodded and smiled. "Absolutely. Come in, and I'll give you the grand tour. It's not much, but it's homey." He showed Roland around the small rooms, which included a combo bedroom and sitting area, walk-in closet, and bathroom. The nonspecific décor was ideal for Roland, and he was relieved it didn't have personal pictures of the family.

"We eat breakfast at six and supper at five. Knock on the adjacent door." He pointed. "You're welcome to join us for both if you like. Cheryl is a wonderful cook." He patted his stomach and smiled. "We're usually not home for the midday meal, so you'll need to fend for yourself. We installed a microwave and mini-fridge if you care to stock it—" He gripped Roland's shoulder. "Sorry, forgot you're broke. Get settled in, shower, and after the volunteers finish, I'll bring you a change of clothes from the church's closet." He glanced at his guest's feet. "And some boots. It looks like you kinda wore those out. You walked all the way here from where?"

Roland lifted one foot and glanced at the sole. "Yes, sir, I did. I couldn't get a ride. It was a long trip from Montana."

The pastor's eyes widened. "Son, you must be tired. I know I am, just hearing that you walked all that distance. It'll be about two hours before I return."

Roland nodded and set his backpack on the floor beside the bed. And then, without warning, tears welled up and spilled down his cheeks. Pastor Eli wrapped him in his arms and let him release all his pent-up emotions.

When they pulled apart, Roland withdrew a hanky from his back pocket and ran it over his face.

"You want to talk?" The pastor gestured toward the sitting area.

He lowered onto one of two recliners. "You're the only person I've met in the last two years who has treated me like a human. A person. A man. Your actions overwhelmed me, and I just—"

"Yep, it's sad we don't have more Christian brothers and sisters showing more love. I wasn't always a pastor and didn't choose this profession. I was chosen. And, yes, at one point, I went kicking and screaming. I wouldn't have gotten here without Jesus. I was a mess with all my lying, cheating, and stealing, and I nearly went to jail. Glad I never indulged in those drugs. I needed money, so I broke into a house…" The pastor shook his head. "I don't know what made me pick that rickety, old house, but I'm convinced I must've been led there. I found an old man waiting in a rocker with a shotgun resting across the chair's arms when I entered. He didn't aim the weapon at me but demanded I sit. You bet I complied. He talked for the next two hours and set me straight about what it meant to be a child of God, what was expected of me as His child, and how to live as a man, husband, and father. My dad died when I was ten, so he never had the chance to instill those values in me." He shook his head again and shrugged one shoulder. "I ran wild, and Mom couldn't control me, and she gave up after a while. I never blamed her because I was way too much to manage."

The pastor held his gaze on Roland, who had sat silent while he shared his personal testimony. "I hope this conversation benefits you as that one did me six years ago. That old man set the gun aside, took me by the hand, and led me to Christ. I surrendered and started trusting Jesus with my destination. It wasn't easy—not then and still isn't now. When you follow Jesus, you sometimes struggle and doubt, but life will improve. Peace permeates your soul—you'll be glad once you see it and feel it. We all have a standing invitation to a purpose and meaning, Roland. It's ours for the asking. Surrender to His direction and trust Him with your destination. It's well worth the fight you endure." Pastor Eli chuckled. "I never knew the old guy's name, but the city demolished the old house the next day." He smiled. "He had to be an angel. Or...." He scratched behind his ear, pondering the 'or.'

Roland ran the hanky over his face again. "Years ago, I asked the Lord into my heart and believed He is the Son of God. Afterward, things started happening beyond my control. I prayed but didn't hear an answer or receive a solution. Then…Dad…." Roland paused.

"Yeah. I'm sorry, son, but He does want His children to be strong for His purpose, and sometimes we'll have struggles that we just don't understand. He is building a better man—a man who can serve Him for others. He has brought you through this last season in life with flying colors. You probably got scarred along the way—maybe more than once—but take heart, He has given you His bread of life to share with others."

Roland sniffed and nodded. "Manna is what I call it."

Eli slapped his back, stood, and headed for the door. He turned, smiled, and eased the door closed as he stepped outside.

Roland bowed his head. "Lord, is this where you want me? Give me the strength to face my brother. In Jesus' name. Amen."

~ Chapter Six ~

Roland relaxed beneath the heavenly flow of hot water and planned to stay underneath it as long as it held out. Living on the streets didn't provide the luxury of showering, and he literally watched people eye him while they'd slink away. He ran a hand over his heavy beard and wished he had a razor. He would need a shave and haircut to be presentable to prospective employers, but his brother was probably still at the center. On second thought, he might get a glimpse of Renee's sister, Jeanne.

After wrestling with the idea, he dried, wrapped a towel around his waist, and waited on Pastor Eli's return with fresh clothes or, at the very least, something without holes. Settled in one of the sitting area chairs, he buried his face in his hands. *How can I face Winston? I'm not ready, but I must eventually talk to him and Renee.*

Roland kept his Bible handy when he needed a Word of encouragement. He mindlessly thumbed through the pages in search of such encouragement, but the years of grief and guilt pummeled his soul. He'd denied the truth too long. *I ran as far as I could.* He shook his head. *No more. No more guilt and shame.*

His fingers stopped on Jeremiah twenty-nine and scanned the scriptures until the words of verse eleven jumped off the page, "For I know the plans I have for you," declares the Lord, "plans to prosper you and not to harm you, plans to give you hope and a future."

Roland dropped to his knees. "I know these words are true because You said them. Thank You for showing me this verse. You never cease to amaze me with Your insight into my life. My doubts are hard on You. Guide Your child in Your direction for my destination—I don't want to continue this same course that I set on my own. I trust You with my life, soul, heart, and future. In Jesus' name. Amen."

Pastor Eli returned with a sack full of clothes, meaning everyone, including Jeanne, had left the center. A wave of something had rushed through him when he saw her. Roland was unsure how to define it—was it her beauty, the way she served others, perhaps a joyous heart when she did? Whatever it was, it intrigued him, and he wanted to know her better.

"Thank you, pastor, for picking these up for me. I feel a lot better since I showered."

"Absolutely. I hope these things fit. I got several shirts and jeans and a pair of boots." Eli pulled a razor off the top of the bag. "Also, I brought a razor in case you decide to shave."

Roland smiled and took the sack. "I don't know how—?" He lowered his chin.

Eli gripped Roland's shoulder. "We won't be left in a place of doubt and despair. We are never alone when we traverse through these struggles of hurt and loneliness, but remember, He won't let us remain in them. Always seek His Word for direction. He's the only one who knows when it's time for you to move into another season of your life."

Tears welled in Roland's eyes, but he swallowed them back. "What I was trying to say and couldn't is, I don't know how to repay you."

"No repayment is required. Just pass on the kindness of Jesus to someone you might see needing a hand up, in dire straits, or just needing compassion. That's all I ask in return, brother. Someday you'll encounter such a person or persons. Remember, your testimony can aid other brothers and sisters, like mine or Winston's."

"Yes, sir. I definitely can do that. Judging by the number of homeless men who sheltered last night and the ones that arrived for a meal, there must be a great need in the community."

"Please call me Eli. After all, I'm not much older than you. Get dressed, and we'll get your hair cut. My friend is waiting. I talked him into staying a little longer."

"Sure, Eli."

Every community needs this kind of pastor and man. Too bad they are so few in the world.

After dressing, Roland and Pastor Eli headed back to the center. Their stroll was initially silent, but Eli clearly had something on his mind.

Eli broke the silence before they arrived at the center. "Roland, we need to find you a job. We'll work on a resumé and feature your best abilities. Is tomorrow soon enough?"

"Why not today?"

"I have this afternoon blocked out to go over tonight's Bible study. I hope you'll join us."

With an open invitation, he'd normally jump at the chance, but he wanted a day of adjustment to get his head straight. What happened that morning at the center continued to weigh heavy on him. He didn't want to be in such a defensive mode around others and have them misconstrued. "Sorry, I don't mean to take up all your time. Tomorrow's fine. When do you want to meet?"

"Come to my office around ten."

"Perfect. While you study your sermon, I'll list my abilities and work experiences. Although take warning, it'll be short. After my stint in the service, I roamed around and took any work I could do."

"No worries, we'll make do. If you recall, our town might be small, but we support the locals in every way, and now you're back home. Many in the community and the church believe in a second chance for all. But don't take their benevolence as a charity. They expect and require hard work and a good work ethic from anyone they employ. No free passes will be given."

"I understand, and I won't disappoint you or them." Roland disliked being the center of attention as others thought he needed charity. He just wanted to be treated fairly as well as a man. "Eli, I changed my mind about tonight, and I'll be in the back row."

"Glad you'll come. You can sit anywhere in the sanctuary. I have an idea. Before the service, I do a short teaching with the youth. Why don't you come early and be my assistant? You don't have to do anything but sit there…unless you feel the Holy Spirit nudging you to help."

The morning had begun like any normal day but soon became a blessing for which Roland would forever be thankful. His heart was overwhelmed by the blessing of a meal, clothes, a shave, a haircut, and a place to lay his head.

After aiding Eli with the youth, Roland returned to his new abode with a sense of peace rivering through him. As darkness shrouded the snow-covered town, Roland swiveled the armchair toward the window, lowered himself, and stretched his legs in front of him. He was exhausted but in a good way. Silence smothered the neighborhood as families retired to their homes and clicked off the lights for the evening. The day came into context.

Everything had been orchestrated—Renee, Winston, Jeanne volunteering, Pastor Eli helping with the youth, now a safe and clean place to lay his head.

Roland couldn't sleep. Too many newfound freedoms embraced him, ones that hadn't been in his life for years. Then the pitter-pat of snow melted as it dripped off the house gutters, a rhythm mirrored his own heartbeat—a slow and steady rate that would remain forever.

As a young girl, Jeanne had welcomed the still, small voice. Now that voice was gone to who knew where. Nightly, she dropped to her knees and prayed. She refused to admit defeat and continued to have faith, not because of the desert she had trekked through but because of the joy of obedience.

During the long day at the center and church where Jeanne and Renee had volunteered, she again saw the Lord's handiwork on display, with the sad faces turning to happy as they partook in a warm meal and a kind word.

Jeanne stretched out all the kinks in her body from the long and rewarding day. A smile lifted on the corner of her lips as she brushed out her long hair, then slipped a gown over her head. Tonight seemed different—in search of how as she settled on top of the quilt and pulled her Bible off the bedside table.

Her thumb fanned across the pages, which fell open to Jeremiah twenty-nine, and a passage stood out like a beacon, verse eleven, "For I know the plans I have for you," declares the Lord, "plans to prosper you and not to harm you, plans to give you hope and a future."

Jeanne closed her Bible and slid off the bed to her knees. "Thank You, Lord. You speak to me in different ways, and tonight I know You haven't forsaken me and my doubts. I just need to be patient with Your journey, not mine. But I still have questions buried in my heart that only You can answer. I'll wait for Your answer, through Your Word or with one of Your servants. In Jesus' name. Amen."

How would she sleep on this night? The day's activities swirled in her head, and the awful memory of what Roland had done earlier to the family sent pangs through her gut.

Finally, heavy lids closed, and she fell into a blissful sleep.

Jeanne dreamed of her brother Henry, older by fifteen years, escorting her down the aisle in a chapel. At the altar stood a man she didn't recognize. A dark shadow covered his face. The man held out his hand, and she accepted it. Confusion swamped her mind about who this man was. Next to her stood her sister, Renee, with her arms full of yellow roses. After Jeanne said I do, she woke up. She clutched her throat, trying to breathe.

"Was this You, Lord telling me about my future? If so, who is the man? I pray he will have You in his heart. That's all I ask. I can deal with anything if You're in the center of my marriage with a man who also loves You. Show me if I become enamored with someone on my path that'll sway my direction away from Your will."

She pulled her Bible off the bedside table, and this time, it fell open to John thirteen, and the passages thirty-four and five were clearly marked. "A new command I give you: Love one another. As I have loved you, so you must love one another. By this, everyone will know that you are my disciples if you love one another."

"Am I harboring any bitterness against my father? I don't hate either of my parents. I'm simply confused about his way of raising his family. I love my parents and don't wish harm to either of them, but why didn't my father give me away in the dream? Are You showing me something?" She swallowed back a tear. "Won't my dad be around when it comes time for me to marry? I hope and pray for his safety and health. Also, I didn't see my mother there—where was she? In Jesus' name. Amen."

Jeanne's eyes grew heavy, and she fell asleep with her hand gripping the passage she read.

~ Chapter Seven ~

Assisting Eli with the youth the previous night at church gave Roland a sense of value—something he hadn't felt in such a long time. Since the day he gave his heart to Jesus, he was secure in knowing fully well his steps were directed, and tonight in the session with the boys was proof enough for him. Before Roland had entered the room with a dozen or so young men, he offered a silent prayer not to say anything to discourage but speak so they'd understand.

And he did just that.

Each young man was given the opportunity to ask questions or join in the lesson. Roland added his perspective on a few comments to aid two boys in understanding part of the passage Eli taught, and to his amazement, his input was encouraging to the boys. Just as he hoped.

Could I teach? I never saw myself as a teacher. Is this my new beginning? Roland rubbed his forehead. He smiled to himself, but then his past etched itself across his mind, and the smile surrendered to a frown. The hope of a new start dangled before him like a carrot enticing a mule to step forward. With the humiliation of a dishonorable discharge, then when released from the military prison, he'd wandered aimlessly across the country searching for answers—answers he knew wouldn't be made known soon. But now, hope sprung within him of a fresh start, even though it was in his hometown.

At an early age, he'd resolved to let the Lord lead him in every circumstance. After leaving home with a knee-jerk reaction, he logged many miles on his feet and heart. One thing was sure: he was led back to his childhood home, so he must do his part after the endless nudge he received the last several months. And today, here he was in his hometown, about to start fresh. When the timing was right, everything would be revealed. For now, he enjoyed the comforts of the soft bed, warm shelter, and hot meals—all thanks to Eli and Cheryl.

Roland thumbed the pages of his Bible. It fell open to Philippians four, and his gaze pinned on the marked passage in verse nineteen, "And my God will meet all your needs according to the riches of His glory in Christ Jesus."

He lowered onto his knees and bowed his head. "I can't ask for anything more than what You've shown and provided me since setting me on this path. Please continue to do so. I hold steadfast to

Your Word and teachings. Thank You, Father. In Jesus' name. Amen."

Roland glanced at the clock above the microwave. Would he have money to buy food to stock the mini-fridge? He didn't want to continue to eat at his host's house. Their benevolence was overwhelming with just a place to live. Pulling the jacket off the peg, he shrugged it on, withdrew a toboggan from the pocket, and dragged it down over his ears. The barber did a good enough job with the haircut, but Roland wasn't accustomed to his ears being so exposed to the weather—he found that out last night when he was in the cold.

After he gathered the completed list of his experiences for the resumé Pastor Eli could create, he clicked the door shut and turned the lock. He needed a job. Nothing short of yet another miracle would do to find employment in this small town—exactly what had been done and continued to do as of late.

The overnight above-freezing temperatures melted most of the snow and ice, leaving the streets somewhat clear, with a few patches on the sidewalks and curbs. With only a few vehicles traversing the road this late morning, Roland nevertheless watched his surroundings—a forced habit from his previous life, although the short walk to the church was uneventful.

Faint memories of Winston and himself as kids played across his mind—snowball fights, snow angels, and sledding were the main activities during their winter breaks from school. “Brother, I hope you haven’t completely disowned me, and our relationship can be repaired.” A heavy sigh billowed from his chapped lips.

With one foot on the church’s bottom step, his gaze followed upward toward the tall steeple. The sun peek from behind a cloud—sunrays jetted as if it backlit the cross while it sliced a beautiful display across the sky. He gasped. Then the cloud covered the sun once more.

Roland swallowed hard, climbed the three steps, and pushed open the side door. A small sign on the wall directed him down a hall to reach the office. As he drew closer, a man’s firm but gentle voice echoed the same passion he had heard as a youth. He stopped short of entering. Easing the door a bit open, he listened. He wanted to hear the entire message now, not on Sunday morning. Was he ready to face the congregation and his family?

Tears flooded his cheeks when the pastor referred to Jesus’ parable in Luke 15 about the prodigal son. *Was this parable about me? No, I didn’t seek adventure, wealth, or the world’s pleasures. I sought to escape the abuse and felt unwanted. What am I doing? I don’t belong with these people.* He turned on his heels and headed toward the door.

“Roland. Glad you made it. Come to my office, and we’ll get started on your resumé.”

He turned and faced Eli. “Pastor, are you sure I’ll be accepted back? I heard you practice your sermon. You're right. I disappointed my family and anyone who associates with me." He lowered his gaze to the pair of boots gifted by the shelter.

"Nonsense. You're a child of God and a brother to all in our church. You don't have to prove anything to anyone. You're loved by Jesus because He is love, not because you're lovable. Remember that when challenges and struggles overwhelm your identity. Take comfort in knowing everyone sins and falls short. He forgave and nailed all your sins when He died on the cross. He said, 'It is finished.' Some people ignore how much He suffered for them, but the plain fact is they don't want to be convicted for their ongoing sins. His death is a reminder, and they can't face reality about His torment and the gruesomeness He withstood on the cross because of them."

Roland shook Eli's hand. "Thank you. Let's get me ready to join the community, church, and, eventually, my family. I've been away too long from all three, but I never let my faith waver. I figured my struggles are for a reason, and He'll reveal everything in His perfect timing. God is good."

Eli smiled. "Yes. He is good all the time. Now, I have a few things to talk over with you. Let's go to my office."

Eli's wife, Cheryl, had left a message with Renee, wanting to have a 'little chat,' as she called it, with Jeanne. Back home in Hopewell, at her church, Jeanne had never heard of a pastor's wife who wanted to visit with a female member unless they needed to be advised about a behavior problem. What was the woman's motive? Jeanne was not a church member here. Was she trying to persuade her to stay in Grove Hill? If that was so, it wouldn't take much. Her summer visits with Renee, Winston, and their two adorable children had tugged at her often. But would her parents agree if she did want to move here? She shook off the nonsense—she was too practical to believe they would, and besides, what would be the reason to stay.

During the previous evening's devotional, she heard the Lord directing her to accept the pastor's wife's invitation. Jeanne smiled inwardly about how she'd been guided differently through His Word or people. She never wanted Him to be silent again.

Renee handed her two papers—directions to Cheryl's house and a grocery list. Jeanne shrugged on her coat and poked both into the pocket. "Be careful on your drive. The streets may have a few patches of ice left. Have a long visit with Cheryl before you head to the store."

"I will. Don't worry, sis." Jeanne drew her into a warm sisterly hug before heading out the door to the car. Renee entrusted her with the vehicle, and she didn't want to give her sister any doubt about her driving abilities. On her way to the car, she noted the chill still hung in the air as a reminder winter had begun a bit early.

Renee had baked all morning to fill a tin container to take along for her visit. She set the cookies in the passenger seat. The delicious aroma of oatmeal raisin cookies filled the car's interior—like being enveloped in cookie heaven.

Following the paper's directions, she cautiously maneuvered through the residential streets and pulled in front of the house bearing the address. She grabbed the tasty treats and headed toward the front door.

As she stepped onto the sidewalk, the northern wind cut through her coat, and she hurried toward the front door. The plain, nondescript front façade and porch were what she had expected since Pastor Eli and Cheryl lived in the church's parsonage. Jeanne had listened intently to one of his sermons on her last summer visit. The pastor said that "no one in this world is beneath him. Instead, we are all equal in the eyes of our Lord." The foyer displayed a beautiful, hand-painted picture of Jesus washing the disciple's feet.

Sister Cheryl's lovely smile greeted her at the front door. "Come in. Good morning, Jeanne. I'm glad you're here. Did you have any problem finding the house? Let me take your coat."

"No trouble at all, ma'am. It's a few miles from my sister's place." Cheryl assisted Jeanne with the jacket and hung it on a peg beside the door. "Thank you for inviting me. I'm not sure why I'm here?" Her brow furrowed, waiting for some sort of corrective response.

"Please call me Cheryl." The woman beckoned her to follow. She trailed behind her hostess to the kitchen. "Renee baked us a treat—oatmeal raisin cookies. I have always enjoyed her cookies with a tall glass of cold milk," she chuckled.

"Oh, how sweet of Renee. I'll thank her with a note. Did you want milk in place of the tea with our treat?"

"No, tea will be fine. I'm not quite used to this kinda weather. Besides, it'll break the chill off my cold bones. It's a little warmer back home, and we never have below-freezing temperatures for long."

"Yeah. The winters here are difficult. They take some getting used to. Renee's been a delight and a blessing to our church and the community. I see her faith growing more each year. I'm sorry about her mother-in-law's passing. How's the family?" She touched Jeanne's arm. "Were you close to Mrs. Bryson?"

Jeanne shook her head. "No, I wasn't, but my sister was. Sometimes they are fine and then other times…." She fiddled with a loose thread on her pink sweater. "Renee nursed her until the end. She shared with me that her last hours were peaceful. Mrs. Bryson…well, just before her passing, she smiled as if Jesus had taken her hand and led her home. My heart broke when her youngest son wasn't there to see her off on her journey." Jeanne smiled and met Cheryl's gaze. "She's truly at home with Jesus."

Cheryl nodded and gestured toward the kitchen table. "Please, have a seat, and I'll get our tea ready." She filled the kettle and set it on the stove. "Have you considered remaining in Grove Hill or returning home anytime soon?"

Jeanne pried off the cookie lid and slid it beneath the container. "I'm not sure yet." She set the tin in the middle of the table and lowered herself onto the chair. "My parents expect me back home to marry a boy from our community—sorry, from our church. But no guy has captured my eye. I've never understood the church's beliefs and traditions, or am I a little rebellious? Either way, I feel more comfortable when I visit your church. Renee tells me that even though both are of the same denomination, our traditions are different. So far, with the limited visits, I've enjoyed your husband's sermons. At home, I feel like I'm being forced to abide by antiquated church laws. Does your church hold to the stringent belief about each child obeying their parents?"

Cheryl turned from the stove with the kettle and a tea box decorated in a brightly colored floral design. She set them next to the cookies and sat across from her. “The commandment you’re referring to does mean we should honor your mother and father. Honoring and obeying are close cousins. When you honor your parents, you will obey them. It’s the same with God. When we honor the Lord through our works that He leads us to do and be compassionate and loving others, we will obey His Word and commandments without a second thought.

“But our works are never a path to heaven. Jesus paid the price for us. We only need to accept Him into our hearts and believe. God loves His children and gives us free will, but we shouldn’t abuse our free will by not honoring and respecting those who He has put over us in life. Now, if you’re referring to being forced to live an oppressive life at the hand of someone abusing you, then that’s altogether different.”

Cheryl gently laid her hand on Jeanne’s arm and pinned her gaze on her. “Are you being abused? Has someone stolen your voice by intimidation, making you fear the consequences of speaking up? Don’t hold back. You can tell me, sister.”

“No, not at all. Growing up in my father’s house, we—I mean us children—were taught that we must obey. Father would quote the commandment when he thought we did something against it. I read that verse for myself one day and read it as honor, not obey. Am I wrong to think he's misquoting the commandment in order to keep a handle on all his children so that we won't stray from the family, or does he want to control us? I'm the last child at home. It makes me think I'm an embarrassment to him because I'm not married yet like my siblings. Never have I caused Dad or Mom any concern over my actions or deeds. That's why I'm confused."

"You will never be left in a place of doubt and despair. Jesus is with us, and we will go through these things, but seek His Word for direction. He's the only one that knows when it's time for you to move into another season of your life." Cheryl patted her hand. "Saying something contradicting your father's or pastor's teachings isn't the best idea. Have you prayed about your apprehensions?"

"Yes, I have, but I'm not getting any answers. I want to talk to Renee about this, but she has a lot on her plate with Winston, the business, and the kids—not to mention the grief they're going through. I don't want to burden her with a lot of silly questions."

"Your questions are not silly. Whatever you're concerned about, He is, too. I think you have some other things happening back home, to let this one interpretation sidetrack you. Let me share with you something in Isaiah forty-three. You probably already know that Isaiah was one of God's prophets and spoke to the Israelites. I'm not quoting verbatim, but the verse said something like, forget the former things and don't dwell on the past. He's making a new thing. Read that chapter in your quiet time and continue to pray, and you'll find the right time to talk with Renee. The woman is smart. Besides, she may have more insight into the family than you're unaware of."

"Yes—"

A soft rap from a nearby door interrupted the conversation. Cheryl held up a finger. "Excuse me." She rose and stepped over to a door that Jeanne had not noticed as an entrance. She clicked the deadbolt, and Roland Bryson appeared on the other side of the threshold with his arms full of clothes.

"Sister Cheryl, may I wash—"

Jeanne turned sideways in her seat, her gaze locked onto a pair of unmistakably familiar blue-violet eyes. Her hand flew to her chest when her heart performed a strange shudder, a shockwave that echoed throughout her body. *Oh, my. What just happened? Never has a man affected me like this. I know him, but does he recognize me?*

~ Chapter Eight ~

Roland's heart swelled with gratitude when Pastor Eli and his wife generously offered him a temporary home—albeit a stranger. During the last few years, no one had extended such benevolence toward him, but he harbored no ill will against anyone as they gave him a wide berth of distance when he strolled past. His grizzly beard and long hair often reminded him of a backwoodsman, along with the stench—he almost gagged himself whenever downwind—so no, he didn't blame anyone for slinking away.

At breakfast, Cheryl insisted he come by and launder his clothes today. Although he had bathed daily since arriving, changing into a fresh set of clothes would be nice. He also needed a clean shirt and jeans for this coming Sunday's church service. The kids would no doubt appreciate it.

The pile of clothes in the room's corner sent up a sour odor that quickly filled the small apartment. He couldn't let the offensive smell drift next door into Eli and Cheryl's living quarters. Inspecting the soiled clothes, he shook them a bit and determined they'd likely need at least two washings before smelling fresh. Regardless of how frayed, they had to be clean and not offend those around him. *Was that the reason Sister Cheryl insisted I wash my clothes today?*

Gathering a full washer load in his arms, Roland knocked on the adjacent door. Cheryl greeted him with her usual smile. "Hello, Roland. Glad you're taking me up on the offer to use our washer. Come on in. I have a visitor this morning." She gestured toward the kitchen table. "You remember Renee's sister, Jeanne?"

He halted at the threshold and stared at the back of Jeanne Adams' head. He'd know her even from behind. And then she swirled around and stood. Her smile captivated him, just as it had at the shelter. He could not take his eyes off her. A breath slowly slipped from his lips. *Jeanne?* Did he say her name aloud? No. Relief flooded over him.

Cheryl's gaze traveled between her two guests a couple of times. Finally, she spoke again, breaking the silence and Roland's frozen stare. "Jeanne, do you remember Winston's brother, Roland?"

Jeanne blinked, bit her bottom lip, and glanced toward Cheryl. "Um…yes. Good to see you. How have you been?"

"Jeanne." This time, he actually spoke her name, and it was like angels playing musical instruments in the heavens. Mentally he shook himself out of the dream he'd been lost in for at least the last three days.

Jeanne's lips pressed together. "Yep, it's me."

What are you doing? This is your brother's wife's sister. "Sorry. I wasn't expecting to see anyone I knew. How have you been?"

Jeanne laughed. "That's what I asked you."

Oh, man, she has the sweetest laugh. "Fine, now that I'm back home." Roland looked at Cheryl. "I'm sorry to interrupt your visit." He'd become momentarily nose-blind to the bundle of dirty laundry, but then the heater kicked on. The resulting whoosh of air sent a revolting stench up his nostrils to remind him why he had visited. "Sister Cheryl, thank you again for allowing me to use the washer this morning. Is it all right now, or should I come back later?"

"Oh, you're not imposing. The laundry room is through there." Cheryl pointed down the hall. "The first door on the right. When you're finished, please join us. We're having tea and a snack. Renee baked a batch of oatmeal cookies."

Roland's eyebrows lifted. "Renee makes the best cookies I've ever tasted. Excuse me, ladies, I'll be back in a flash." He chuckled and hurried off. He wanted to glance back and steal a glimpse at Jeanne, but that might be too obvious. He'd be at the table in a few minutes and could take in her gorgeous smile again. As he crammed his clothes in the washer, the two women's conversation floated into the laundry room.

"Jeanne, will you get an extra cup and saucer for Roland?"

"Sure. But, Sister Cheryl, I better leave before he returns. Roland needs to have a conversation with Winston and Renee before I do. I feel like I'm betraying my brother-in-law and sister. After all, he came home to see them, not me."

"He will, so don't worry one bit. Give him time. Baby steps. We can talk more later about your situation. Remember, what we do and say is heard, and our actions affect others. Keep praying for the right time to talk to Renee. She's more understanding than you know and a wise woman."

"Thank you. I will."

"Now, let's sit and enjoy your tea and a cookie. Not to mention the good conversation with my new houseguest."

Roland clicked the washer to the correct setting, and images pummeled his mind from days earlier when Jeanne served meals and interacted with his niece and nephew at the shelter. Her sweet smile was the same one she had offered him moments earlier. *Genuine heart. Is she married, have a boyfriend? Does she live here?* Roland shook his head. *She's Renee's kid sister. Stop it. Now.*

Before entering the kitchen, he froze at the doorway when he overheard Cheryl talking to Jeanne. The word 'situation' impaled straight into his gut. *Was she in trouble? Or, even worse, had she sinned?* The impulse to find out more swirled through his mind. But it was not his business. He chided himself for eavesdropping.

To ensure the ladies heard him returning, he cleared his throat. "Thank you, Sister Cheryl, for your invitation. I love Renee's baking. Whoever taught the woman how to cook did an excellent job. I don't know how she did all the housework and cooking when Dad got ill." A glower creased his forehead. Something heavy had fallen across his heart. Images of his dad inundated him, and the same something sent a shiver down his spine. Not wanting anyone to witness this unfavorable side of himself, least of all Jeanne, he stared at the cookie tin and waited for the invitation to help himself.

Cheryl gestured. "Please have a seat. Did you want tea or milk with your treat?"

"Tea, thank you."

He claimed the chair across from Jeanne, the ideal spot to take in her beauty and close enough to have an intimate conversation if Cheryl left the room.

Cheryl filled his cup with hot water and pointed at the floral tea box. "I have a variety. Help yourself."

The various flavored little baggies were lined up like rows of soldiers waiting for marching orders. He perused the selection and glanced at Jeanne. "What did you pick?" One of his eyebrows twitched, waiting for a response. *Surely, I'm not flirting.*

Jeanne's earlier confident tone now turned shy. "The green tea."

After he spied the same tea, he flashed her a grin. "I'll try the same." *Man, you* are *flirting. Stop it.*

"Jeanne, have you heard this young man has decided to stay in the community? Eli is helping him find a job." Cheryl took a sip from her cup. "I really think you'd be an excellent youth minister at our church, Roland. Eli confided in me about how terrific you were with the kids—a natural teacher and leader, answering all their questions. We've been searching for the right person to fill the position for quite a while."

"Thank you, Sister Cheryl. Your vote of confidence means a lot. I don't know where or what God has planned for me. But I'll keep praying about His will for my life and the path He's set me on now that I'm home." His chin lifted, and his gaze met Jeanne's. *Lord, I need a little help. Her eyes are so...so beautiful.* Then she smiled. His heart seemed set on pounding right out of his chest.

"Jeanne, when are you leaving for home?"

Her gaze shot over to Cheryl. “I’ll be going home a week from this Thursday. My parents expect me back so I can start my new life.”

Oh, good, conversation about Jeanne. Please, tell me more about you. Wait! Did I hear that right...going home? New life? Was she married or engaged? No, no, no. Agony reeled within Roland’s gut. He found a woman he’d fallen in love with in a matter of seconds, and now she is leaving.

Neither Renee nor Winston spoke about Roland often, except for a prayer or two for safety and to bring him home. Yet something about him nudged at Jeanne’s soul, and she wanted to know him better. All she knew about him was that he’d just turned eighteen when he left home and joined the army.

Now Jeanne sat across from the man whom she had spent countless hours praying for—most recently, last night. She struggled to understand why he’d left the family and community. What happened? Was he running away from something, like her?

She couldn’t forget those gorgeous blue-velvet eyes after their first meeting when his family arrived in Hopewell for Renee's wedding. Back then, she had a silly schoolgirl crush on him despite having limited contact. The other day at the center, he'd captured her attention again, even though his grungy appearance was less than appealing.

After Roland started his laundry and returned, the three settled at the table for a hot cup of tea. When Sister Cheryl spoke about Jeanne going home to Hopewell, something flashed across his face, and a noticeable change took place in his demeanor. She wanted to understand his sudden expression change. Had something happened during the homeless years he suffered or his stint in the army? Had he perhaps sinned? He was certain to have had unpleasant experiences. Did she want to know? What would she talk to him about or him with her? They had nothing in common.

Cheryl's innocent question was a strident reminder to Jeanne, one that sent a painful streak of reality through her mind. Something nudged at her, a longing to stay here in Grove Hill, a resistance to the idea of returning to Hopewell—not now, when spring filled her heart, even though winter would be upon the land soon.

Jeanne hung on to every word Roland said about last Wednesday night's youth group meeting. His appearance transformed from sad to happy when speaking of the experience, and his smile lit up places in her heart she'd considered locked away for no man to capture. The men back home never interested her, and she cringed at the idea of living in a loveless marriage. None of her siblings went down that path. Instead, they all fell in love like Jeanne longed to do. But if she ever finds a moment to ask her sister's advice about all of it, will Renee tell her that she must marry through the church like their father wants?

Her father's steady demands to get married kept her away, so she avoided him. Would he arrange a marriage while she visited Renee? Surely not.

In the evenings quiet, just before she drifted off to sleep, running away often crossed her mind. But now she'd seen how Roland returned home—his unkempt clothes and body odor, not to mention his heart-rending expression of being spiritually crushed. No telling how a homeless female would be treated. Abused? Beaten? Perhaps even killed. No. That notion sent pangs through her tummy, and she dismissed going down that path.

Without realizing it, she fell into easy conversation with Sister Cheryl and Roland when she told them about her snow angel and her rambunctious niece and nephew. Giggles spewed between her lips, and she hoped she didn't appear too silly. Then she conveyed her desire to study counseling for young girls.

After a while, Sister Cheryl excused herself and left the room. Silence fell between Jeanne and Roland. The shy boy she'd met at Renee and

Winston's wedding had vanished. A more confident young man smiled at her. But she couldn't think of a thing to say. What was wrong with her?

Jeanne ran a finger around the rim of her cup and met Roland's gaze. "Are you going to meet with Winston soon?" She bit her lower lip. How could she ask such a question? That was not her business.

He glanced down the hall and then lowered his chin. "I will. I'm not sure when. It's hard for me to face my brother. He and Renee took on so much, and I'm ashamed of my actions."

She wanted to lay her hand on his to offer comfort and perhaps ease the pain-stricken expression on his face. But that kind of gesture would definitely be too forward. Besides, he might react negatively. "Roland, I'm sorry, this isn't my business. But to be honest, he loves you and wants you home. I don't know why you left or stayed away so long." She held up her hand to halt his response. "You don't need to share with me any of your reasons. Just please, believe me, your family loves you. They will forgive you. All they want is to have you safely back in the family."

He met her gaze, and his eyes softened. "Before I ask for their forgiveness, I needed to know they would. Thanks. I appreciate you telling me how they felt. It will make it a bit easier. Leaving back when I was so young was a mistake…I was naïve and should have talked to Winston. You know Dad had a brain tumor. It made him do and say cruel things. I didn't blame him. It was the cancer, and... When I was in the service, I did something against the rules. So they put me in jail. People kinda shy away from me when they find out. Did you know I went to jail?"

"No. I won't ever treat you in that way, Roland. We all make mistakes. If you need to talk, call me, or better yet, text. My phone stays on during the night beside my bed. Things often burden my heart and, well.... I'm not saying my problems compare to yours, but I still have them, and I know they can weigh heavily on your soul. I won't be in Grove Hill long, but we can talk and text while I'm here...I'd like you to reach out to me when I go home, please."

"Thanks, Jeanne. I'd like that. But...can't do it without your number." A crooked little grin flashed on Roland's lips.

Jeanne snatched a piece of paper and pen from the middle of the table, scribbled her cell number, and passed it to him. His fingers brushed hers when he accepted the note, and something akin to a lightning bolt trailed up one finger into her arm and straight to her heart. *Oh, my.*

He folded the paper and slid it into his shirt pocket just as Cheryl returned.

~ Chapter Nine ~

The washer buzzed at the most inopportune moment, and as if on cue, Roland's smile faded. With the ugly reminder pulling him away, questions plagued his mind. Chiefly, when would he get a chance to chat with this incredible woman? He relished the private conversation with Jeanne. Too bad it couldn't last forever.

Roland couldn't recall the last time he had a meaningful discussion with any woman. The moment he sat at the table, all nervousness vanished. He was utterly enthralled with Jeanne's smile, the tilt of her head when she listened, and her musical laughter. All of it quieted his soul. Whatever she did and everything she said captured his heart in the palm of her pretty little hands. He knew it from the beginning and didn't even want to resist.

When he secured Jeanne's phone number into the top shirt pocket near his heart, her lips parted, and he could swear a gasp gushed between them.

Reluctantly, he excused himself, stepped into the laundry room, pulled out the wet clothes, and examined them. The load needed at least one more cycle to release the stink and embedded dirt. He stuffed the clothes back inside and dumped in more detergent. *This load might do the trick. If not, I don't know what to do. Maybe Cheryl will have a suggestion. Get the lead out, Roland, and get back to the ladies…to Jeanne.*

During his haste to return, he didn't hear Jeanne and Sister Cheryl leave the kitchen. When the women weren't in sight upon his return, a sharp pain ripped through his gut. Female voices echoed from the living room, so he followed them.

Jeanne stood by the door with her hand on the knob. A knot clogged his throat. "Um, are you leaving so soon? Weren't you going to tell me?"

She lifted her gaze to meet his and blessed him with another beautiful smile. "Yes and no. Of course, I wouldn't leave without telling you. I was waiting for you, but I have errands to do for Renee. I'll see you on Sunday morning…I hope."

He nodded. His hand gently patted his shirt pocket, where he stowed her number. "Sure. Oh, I was thinking. Will you help me with the youth group on Sunday and again Wednesday night? I'm working out a lesson about Jesus' first miracle for this Sunday's lesson. On Wednesday, we'll gather in one of the empty rooms and try a little harmony on a few hymns. Can you carry a tune?"

She shyly winked as if to reward him for his thoughtfulness, her hostess being none the wiser.

"Yes. That gives me a reason to come to church on those days instead of packing. Thanks for asking me. Please, will you share the information with me? I don't want to stumble through either the lesson or the hymns. That wouldn't give the kids a good impression. So…I guess we'll talk later. Bye."

"For sure. Thanks again." His heart did three flips when she agreed. He wanted to spend every waking minute with Jeanne. Studying together would have to suffice until he could find another excuse to see her.

Jeanne nodded to Cheryl and left. The impulse to peek out the window overwhelmed his common sense, but then he checked himself. That kind of behavior would be too obvious in front of Sister Cheryl.

Cheryl gestured toward the kitchen. "Please have another cup of tea with me."

Roland managed a half-smile and accepted her invitation. Memories of Jeanne and their conversation rambled through his head. He'd spoken about stuff he swore never to breathe to anyone other than a pastor, but he only told her how his father changed, the pain he inflicted, and his stent in jail. The worst would be told another day—another chat when he was ready to reveal more. Would she tell Renee or, worse, Winston?

What could I offer her…nothing? Sweaty palms rubbed on the front of some other man's pants that he wore, and he exhaled a shuddery breath. *Lord, do You have a plan for Jeanne and me…I mean, the two of us? I have never imagined being with such an angel. The moment I saw her at the center, it was like an invisible force encircled my heart, claiming it only for her. Is this real love? Please direct my steps and not let me blow my chances with her.*

Cheryl's voice pulled him from his muse. "Are you all right, Roland?"

"Sorry. What did you say?"

"Did your clothes not come clean on the first wash?"

He lifted his cup of cold tea and took a large gulp. His nose scrunched. "No, ma'am. I ran them through again. Do you mind?"

"Not at all. Whatever is necessary to get them clean. Eli mentioned he was stopping by the shelter to see if any more clothes were donated in your size. So he may have a set for you later today. Do you mind having to wear secondhand?"

"No, ma'am."

Cheryl rose to stop the shrill whistle of the teapot. She brought it to the table, filled Roland's cup, and lowered herself onto the chair. "It was nice of Renee to bake the cookies and for Jeanne to bring them over today. I like her." She lifted her cup and peered over the rim. "Do you?"

"It sure was nice of them both." Roland shifted in his seat, and his palms grew moist again.

"I hope Jeanne will stay longer in Grove Hill. Maybe permanently. But I suppose her family misses her and wants her back home."

He ran his finger around his cup's rim and sighed. "I guess so."

"Have you and Eli talked about the youth minister position? I really think you'll be the person to guide these kids. It carries with it a small part-time wage. If you take the job, it'll start you on the road to a new beginning. Please consider the opportunity and pray about it."

"Eli did suggest the job to me. But I'm not sure if I'd be accepted into the church. You know my story?" He met her gaze, searching for judgment, and spotted none.

"Not all of it, but I saw how you were with the kids. You have Jesus in your heart, Roland. Regardless of what sins we have committed in the past, we are forgiven. He loves His children, and you're one of them. Please don't permit the enemy to rake you over the coals with your past by making you doubt your potential.

"Roland, one of the Lord's prophets, Isaiah, spoke to the Israelites in chapter forty-three about forgetting the former things and not dwelling in the past. God's doing a new thing. Take some time and read those passages. You'll find He is speaking to you and will direct your steps. The Lord has a plan for each of us. Just listen to His voice and follow what He has for you. Pray on it, listen, and obey."

"I will. Thank you. You don't know how much I appreciate you and Eli helping me, even if it's temporary."

"You're welcome. You can stay here as long as you like. I'm confident He has great plans for you. Perhaps she'll stay too."

He lifted a quizzical brow. "Who?"

Cheryl laughed. "Jeanne, of course."

He looked down at his secondhand clothes again and whispered. "I can only hope so."

Breakfast had been the same every morning since Jeanne arrived. She could tell when the children were finished eating when banter from her niece and nephew filled the table. She loved hearing the little ones and relished their bond.

Jeanne spun a spoon in a bowl of oatmeal, scooped up a raisin, stared at it, and then dropped it back inside the dish. Marie licked off a glob of oatmeal and shook her spoon at her brother. "Stop it," she warned for the second time.

The children's teasing faded into the background. *Will Renee understand, or perhaps…? No, Sister Cheryl assured me I wasn't being silly or overly sensitive.*

Laughter trilled throughout the room. Brice shoved Marie's shoulder, and she tittered on her seat and released a shrill. Drawn from her muse, Jeanne gasped and lurched forward to grab Marie before she crashed onto the floor. Brice beat Jeanne by inches when he latched hold of his sister's arm and pulled her back onto the seat in time to prevent a disaster.

Renee's dark eyebrows lifted. "Okay, I guess you guys are through eating. You may go to the playroom. Please leave the door open."

Jeanne admired how she lovingly handled her children—never demanding or being forceful. Where had she learned this from? It surely wasn't from their parents. Perhaps she'd seen it in Winston's mother. Then again, maybe she'd learned by trial and error, growing with each experience.

Brice and Marie stopped before exiting the room. Turning, the children smiled, waved at her, and then skipped down the hallway. When Roland hadn't returned home after Marie's birth, Winston remodeled his brother's bedroom into a playroom. The space was ideal for closing the door when company came or for play dates with other friends. Renee and Winston didn't believe in their children having a lot of toys, so the room had more room for playing tag or floor games when the outside weather wasn't ideal.

Jeanne gathered the dishes off the table and carried them to the sink. She rolled up her sleeves, washed and dried the last dish, then turned to Renee. "Can we talk?"

"How about another cup of coffee while we chat?"

"Sure." *It'll give me something to focus on while I try to confide in Renee if I cannot look into her eyes.*

Renee topped off their coffee cups and claimed the chair across from her.

Jeanne added sugar and creamer while she ran the rehearsed scenario through her mind. She sighed and gathered enough courage to drop the question onto her older sister. "Ree, have either our brothers or you ever felt like Dad held a tight fist over us kids growing up? I mean, Dad has been more..."

The dry lump in Jeanne's throat grew by the second. She gulped down a good amount of coffee and nodded at Renee before continuing. "I ran across a Bible passage that kinda conflicts with what Dad has taught us over the years. I figured he wouldn't intentionally misquote or use His Word for selfish reasons. Remember when he repeatedly counseled us about how we must *obey* him and Mom? The verse is written as *honor*. It conflicts with Dad's and Mom's version. When I visited Sister Cheryl, I spoke to her about it, and she suggested I talk to you. I've been trying ever since I arrived in Grove Hill, but—"

"I hoped and prayed you'd share what was on your heart, sis. Go ahead. I'm listening."

Jeanne nodded. "Has Dad taken the obey and honor too far? Since graduating high school, they have pressured me to marry quickly and leave the house." Her steady hands now shook while she stirred the coffee. *Please, help me, Ree. I need to understand why. Nothing makes sense in what they're doing. You're the only one who can.* "What do you think? I mean, is it possible…I was mistaken, and Mom and Dad don't want me?" She pinned a stare on Renee.

"Have you prayed what's in your heart?"

"Yes. Months and months now, but I haven't received an answer yet. But I'm not giving up on prayer or on Him answering."

Renee tapped a finger on the side of her cup. "Don't overreact, sis. Your prayers are heard. Just because we question something doesn't mean He's abandoned us. And neither has Mom or Dad. They love you, and no, you're not a mistake. Give the Lord time, and He'll answer you."

"All right. Tell me the truth. Have I hurt you in any way in speaking to Cheryl before I talked to you, sis?'

"Not in the least. Sister Cheryl is there to guide us through the valleys we seem to get bogged down in." Renee swallowed and continued. "You are unaware of some things… Henry almost ruined his life years ago. You were incredibly young when it happened. The family never spoke about it, and

I won't now. He repented. You know that means to change your mind, right?"

"Yes. I found the definition online while researching the passage I'm concerned about. With all sin, we need to change our minds about the direction we're headed in."

"Henry quickly straightened up, and that's when Dad got strict. You never got the freedom he gave us older children before that occurred. Sis, you're the last child at home. I think the folks are tired and ready to start their retirement years. Remember, they've been raising children for over thirty-five years. Dad took a grip on us children, so we won't stray from God or His Word. He has tried to protect your soul like our Heavenly Father does. I'm certain Dad had many conversations with Jesus on our behalf. After Ephesians 6:1, where the passage states children should obey, verse four tells fathers not to exasperate the children. So it swings both ways with obey and honor, but we all need to trust each other. When you go home, be honest with Dad and Mom. Do you have any bitterness against our parents?"

"None. Just confusion. I understand more now why Mom and Dad raised us that way. They were blessed with children and the responsibility of guiding us through His precepts, so we won't stray. But I want to love the man I marry, attend college, and have a family. I'll talk to them.

"Dad's teachings about graduating high school and getting married to the first eligible man around are definitely not for me. Renee, you fell in love with Winston, and look at you guys—you have a rock-solid marriage and children—you're happy. Am I wrong to want those things too?"

"Not at all, sister. But you'll have to compromise on the college thing. Dad won't pay your tuition, so you must get a job. Is there anyone in Hopewell you're interested in as a potential husband?"

Jeanne's lips flattened into a thin line, and she shook her head. "The guys back home are immature and goofy. The type of men I don't want. Their attitudes are subjective and demanding. Whenever I dated a guy my age, he expected me to marry him the next day."

Renee laid her hand on Jeanne's. "Winston and I have talked about you permanently moving in here with us. We'd love for you to stay. Think about our offer and pray. We never want to leave the Lord out of any decision. We must obey His direction and His plan for us. Next Thursday, you'll be going home. I've got a suggestion. Go home and get the rest of your clothes and return. Winston and I will talk to Mom and Dad. Remember, little sister, the Lord will make a way." Renee smiled and squeezed her hand. "Are you interested in someone in Grove Hill?"

Jeanne grinned. "I am. But how can I be sure he wants to be with me or if he's the man God has placed in my path?"

"Listen to that small, still voice...He's speaking to you, perhaps in other ways. If any man has Jesus in his heart, his actions will reflect them. He might be the man to wait for, and he'll be directed in your path. Dozens of things are done daily that we are unaware of, and most don't come to light right away, but one day they will. Then you'll see His purpose. The same with a verse. We read the same passage several times, and it meant little to us at the moment. But then, one day, it opens up to you, becomes crystal clear, and you totally understand the meaning. This holds true with everything the Father does for us."

Jeanne nodded. "He does, and I'm hoping he's the man God has placed in my life. Thanks, sis. I'm glad you showed me a little of what I didn't know about our parents and the reason for their actions. I was confused by that passage and hoped our parents weren't taking the commandment out of context. Thanks for your offer of coming to live here with you guys. I'd like that very much so."

"You're welcome. You will be led in the right direction and toward your purpose. I have an idea what He's doing." Renee held up her hand, stopping her. "I'm not revealing it until it happens."

The women shared a giggle.

~ Chapter Ten ~

A burst of frigid wind blasted through Roland's jacket, cutting him to the bone. He snugged the collar of the thin coat tighter and quickened his steps toward his brother's house. His icy fingers grazed his neck, sending a chill down his spine. He searched for gloves in the coat pockets but found nothing but lint—not even his warm toboggan for his ears. When Sister Cheryl relayed his brother's message earlier, Winston agreed to a meeting. He hurried out the door so fast that he mistakenly plucked the wrong coat off the peg.

Roland sent a silent prayer upward to open Winston's and Renee's hearts and accept him back into the family fold. Glad the Lord nudged him enough yesterday during his morning prayers to finally contact Winston. He had left a message on their home phone with the pastor's number.

Somehow, he sensed it was crucial that he arrive on time for the impending reunion, and he wanted nothing to derail him from talking with his family. His father's illness replayed in his head with each stride on the two-mile walk. Roland gripped his ears, trying to reject the words and actions during those days, weeks, and months that he desperately wished had not happened, but all the wishing in the world couldn't change the facts. They did happen.

Roland stopped in his tracks and bowed his head. "Heavenly Father, You said that when we go through trials while we are in the weeds, we must depend upon You. I'm sorry for not relying on Your Fatherly guidance back then and not trusting You, but now I do with my whole heart. Please let my brother and sister-in-law forgive me." Tears streamed off his cheeks. "The guilt of what I did to You by not relying on You to see me through has burdened my soul. Forgive me. I need Your grace from this mounting shame and condemnation, so I can run the race You've set before me. Amen."

The large house he had called home for eighteen years came into sight within a block. The earlier chill that bit at him calmed, and a bead of sweat dotted his forehead. Was it the weather or his nerves? He ran a jacket sleeve across his forehead and straightened his shoulders. He had dawdled long enough.

The two parked cars in the driveway must be Winston's and Renee's. His brother had taken good care of his parent's property. Before Roland's untimely departure, the house needed lots of work. Money was tight with his father's surgeries and treatments. *Thanks, brother, for agreeing to meet me.* He swallowed back the lump and lifted shaky knuckles to knock on the door. *Can't turn around now.*

An unnerving creak echoed when the front door opened—he recalled that same irritating noise before he ran away. Roland held a tense grin and hoped for the best, which in his reckoning was forgiveness. This is all he would expect. "Um. Hello, Winston."

Tears flooded down his brother's cheeks. He grabbed Roland's shoulders and pulled him into a tight hug. "Thank you, Lord, my brother is home." Winston's hoarse whisper revealed the depth of his emotion.

Roland melted into his arms. *Everything may be all right after all.*

"Let's go into the house. Renee put a pot of coffee on. I hope she has some of those cookies left."

When Roland stepped over the threshold, his stomach tightened, and a flurry rippled through his gut. Memories slammed him head-on—countless lectures in this very room on how to be a good man, husband, and father when the time came. The bad incidents in his mind, and oh, how he wished they would evaporate, even the good stuff. Winston and Renee remained in the large home when his mom passed away. Thankful he didn't have to live here anymore.

Renee greeted Roland with a warm hug. "Glad you're home, brother."

"Me too, sis."

"Please sit." Renee filled three cups and set a container of oatmeal raisin cookies in the center of the table. Even though he boasted how marvelous Renee's cookies were days earlier, his stomach could not manage one bite, but he might ask for a whole batch to take home.

After a few sips, Roland began. "Winston, Renee, I know you're disappointed in me. I ran like a wounded dog before Dad's funeral. I need to explain." He hauled in a breath…one more, and then continued. "When Dad got sick, his entire attitude changed. Day after day, I prayed for his recovery, but he didn't get any better. Instead, he became more volatile and turned violent toward me…." His knuckles whitened around the cup.

Renee laid her hand on his arm. "Take a breath and start again when you're ready." Her empathetic tone encouraged him. White knuckles returned to normal. He shot her a grateful look and continued.

"Several months before he passed away, he…," Roland scrubbed his face with his hand. "This only ever happened at the shop, but he took a razor strap to my back four times. My back bled, and I still have physical and mental scars from the beatings. What really broke my heart was when Mom came in one day and witnessed the brutality, and she did nothing. I felt all alone and abandoned by both my parents. I thought the worst—that she'd agreed with his punishment—and I never knew what I did wrong."

Tears streamed down both Renee's and Winston's faces. Roland's sob-filled voice continued. "After you came home, brother, I figured things would improve, but they didn't. The tumor had taken over Dad's personality. Mom must've known it, but she never mentioned to me the incident she saw at the shop. I kept silent because I didn't want you to think badly about our parents. Did she talk about it to you guys?"

They shook their heads.

"Winston, after Dad died, guilt besieged me hard."

"Why, brother?"

"Daily, I'd prayed Dad would be healed. When he wasn't getting better, and all medical possibilities were exhausted, I prayed that Jesus would take him home." Roland lowered his chin, unable to look his brother in the eye. "Shame nearly drowned me. Can you and Renee forgive me for leaving you to care for Mom and the business? I didn't get your letter about Mom's passing until three weeks after her funeral. Then, I had no reason to hurry back home."

Renee and Winston pushed back from the table and knelt on either side of his chair. Two pairs of arms comforted him. In a matter of moments, tearful sobs filled the quiet kitchen.

"Brother, we forgave you a long time ago. We love you and want you home. I'm sorry you thought you couldn't talk to me about the torment you experienced. Please forgive us. We didn't see what was happening to you." Winston held his gaze with Roland's. "Forgive yourself, little brother. Don't harbor any guilt or bitterness toward our parents."

"I've been trying to forgive myself for leaving while also taking on the guilt of the abuse. I figured I was a bad son and a disgrace as a man because Dad punished me. Otherwise, why would he do such a horrible thing?"

Renee's sincerity lay across his soul like a soft, warm blanket on a wintry night. "Stop thinking those things about yourself. Look what you did in the service when that officer tried to assault that woman. No telling what would've happened to her if you hadn't stepped in to stop the assault. Honestly, Roland, you did nothing wrong. Neither did Dad nor Mom. The disease turned a gentle, sweet man into a monster. Your mom told me many times about how her husband had changed. I never knew what she was talking about, and now it all makes sense. Winston and I love you. You have a family. Please consider staying in Grove Hill."

"I love you too." He absorbed her gentle pat on his shoulder like water on a parched tongue, then returned to his planned speech topics. "After leaving the service, I wandered the country aimlessly, trying to find any sort of life. Even though I stayed on the streets, God shielded me through my journey and led me back home. He has a purpose for me here. I went to our parents' graves and forgave them when I arrived. I asked for their forgiveness too. I hope the Lord relayed my request to them."

Winston pulled an envelope off the table, nodded, and handed it to his brother. "I'm certain He has, and they are thrilled to no end about the news. Mom gave me a letter before she passed. She said if I ever saw you again, I ought to give it to you. I promise I haven't read it." Winston placed the envelope in Roland's hand and cupped his around them. "Thanks for coming home. You have put my heart at ease."

"I'll go into the living room and read it in private." Roland glanced at the envelope, and a tear landed on his name on the front. He sniffed and quickly bit back the next tear, which was on the verge of escaping.

"Before you go, will it be all right if we pray for you, brother?"

"I'd like that very much."

The three stood. They joined hands and closed their eyes, then Winston began. "Heavenly Father, we stand before You to uplift my brother, Roland. You have set his feet onto a path of Your choosing. Thank You. Whatever, wherever, and for however long the journey will be, fill him with joy, love, and grace as Your servant. Please continue to show us where and when we can help others—the downtrodden, the hungry, the lonely, and any others we can exhibit Your love to. In Jesus' name. Amen."

Roland opened his eyes. The Lord's love permeated his soul in a way he had never felt before. *Thank You, Jesus. I wish Jeanne were here to share in Your joy, Lord.*

"I'll be back in a minute." He rushed out before he completely lost all composure. Leaning against the living room wall, his trembling hands unfolded the paper.

My dear son, I know how disappointed you were in me that day. I saw it in your eyes. No doubt you are still disappointed. My heart broke for you and your father on that terrible day. The man who stood over his child with a horrible razor strap wasn't the man I had married and with whom I had raised two loving and caring sons. All I can say is I'm sorry. Please forgive me for failing to be the mother you deserve. Please try to understand that I, too, had to face the demon that took control of your father during his illness. I wish we could've discussed it to lighten your burden. Since your sudden departure, I often wanted to tell Winston and Renee why you left, but I couldn't face the pain and heartache it would inflict. They didn't need to have that image of your father or of your personal pain.

I don't blame you for leaving, son, but I pray Jesus stays in your heart. He won't abandon you—

not like I did. Trials strengthen us for His Kingdom. He whispered in my ear about your life only last night (as I write this letter). "Roland, will influence those around him and lead many to salvation."

Son, I love you and pray you will forgive me and harbor no bitterness.

I believe God. You always had a heart for the Lord, which showed in everything you did. Goodbye, my sweet baby son. If you return in time for my homegoing, I will enjoy seeing your handsome face again. If not, I understand, and I'll see you when we meet in heaven. Jesus, Dad, and I will welcome you with open arms. Always remember He has set your path. Just listen to His still, small voice and obey. I love you always. Mom.

Roland wiped away more tears with his sleeve and lowered to his knees. *Heavenly Father, thank You for bringing me home. Thank You for my mother's letter. Could you maybe...please tell her that I already forgave her and Dad? No bitterness remains in my heart. I love them both dearly. Thank You for giving me a path to walk and for the abundance of Your love and guidance these last few months. I look forward to the future that Mom said You have for me. And for the first time in years, I feel Your peace. In Jesus' name, I pray. Amen.*

Roland neatly folded the letter and tucked it into his pocket. He returned to the kitchen and sat beside Winston. Heel clicks from the hallway door suddenly stopped. Roland looked up with red, swollen eyes. *Jeanne.* His smile widened as he drank in her beauty.

~ Chapter Eleven ~

"Two more days, and I'll get to see Roland, but what's better is that we get to talk." Jeanne peeked through the bedroom window blind and eyed her niece and nephew playing amiably in the backyard. Brice's big brother persona was obvious to his sister, or could it be bossiness? Even though Marie shook a spoon at him earlier, stating that very thing—no, not this kindhearted little man.

Jeanne held back a giggle as the little girl bounced on her toes. "Please…please, push me in the swing, brother."

He nodded and helped her onto the seat. The little girl sailed higher and higher, and then after the next shove, Marie almost knocked Brice to the ground when he moved too slowly, getting out of her way. He stepped aside quick as a flash of lightning after his next push. Lesson learned.

The cold breeze from the north changed direction and brought in warmer temperatures. Puddles were everywhere in the backyard. *Surely the kids will stay out of the mud and track nothing into the house.* She giggled at the thought. A boy was playing outside. What made her think puddles and boys didn't mix? Her older brothers often tracked mud into their home in Hopewell, and cleaning the floors was her chore. She would stand guard at the back door to ensure no one trampled across one board with muddy or dirty shoes, but they got wise and detoured through the front door.

Her questions about marriage, having a family, and the other reason for her fast get away from home, the misinterpreted Bible verse, all remained at the forefront of her thoughts on the visit. Would she marry a man who wanted children? She'd love to have at least three, two boys and a girl. But how could she marry without love? Thoughts for a later day. Right now, her goal to attend college and work alongside children was important. Miserable doubt reared its ugliness the closer she came to going home, but between now and then, she must stick with the life-changing decision and hoped it was the Lord's chosen path. If not, she was certain He'd guide her steps in an alternative direction.

Jeanne flipped the blind shut and sat on the bed. "Roland," she whispered and closed her eyes, remembering their visit at the pastor's house. He'd cleaned up nicely and looked far better than when she first saw him at the center. Gone was the unattractive, messy beard. The man had no idea how glad she'd been to see his handsome face, and he looked much younger. His gorgeous blue-violet eyes, strong jawline, and sweet smile held her captive while they chatted. But then he shared why he had left home years before, and the pain in those striking eyes nearly crushed her.

When he asked if she would assist him at church and the youth group, he'd offered her a ray of hope that he was interested, and then again, wretched doubt seeped into her spirit. "Or was he simply being nice? Maybe no one else volunteered. After all, the class did need two teachers. But he promised to call me, and he hasn't even texted. What if he changed his mind?" *Stop thinking that way, Jeanne.* "He'll contact me soon."

She glanced at her phone for the umpteenth time—and the morning wasn't even over. A heavy sigh escaped, and then she questioned whether he even had a cell phone. "If he wants me to help, he'll find a way of contacting me. Better get going. Chores wait for nothing."

Jeanne shut the bedroom door and trudged the length of the hall toward the kitchen. She planned to treat the kids to the ice cream parlor after lunch. But first, she had promised Renee to help with the laundry. Marie and Brice would tromp through the back door any minute, hungry.

As she neared the kitchen, a prominent male voice came into earshot. *That's Winston. Why is he home? Is something wrong?* She stopped in the doorway, surprised to find Roland, her sister, and her brother-in-law at the table chatting. All eyes turned toward her. "Um. I'm sorry to intrude." Her gaze met Roland's, and she froze in place, unable to move forward or backward. The floor held her shoes captive. She tried to force herself to turn around, but nothing happened. *Please help me, Renee. Say something, 'cause I can't.*

Renee's voice broke through and brought her out of the beguilement. "Jeanne, it's all right. You can stay."

"I, I, …all right. You guys pretend I'm not here." She gave a little wave, padded to the cupboard, removed a glass, and turned on the faucet.

Renee met her at the sink. "Come sit with us," she whispered. "We're all together as a family again." Jeanne nodded, refilled the glass she'd barely drunk, and Renee accompanied her to the table.

Jeanne lowered herself across the table from Roland. Wide-mile smiles plastered across both brothers' faces. Their happiness filled Jeanne with peace. She'd prayed daily for this to happen, and now it had. Joy seemed to ooze from his soul, which is exactly what she longed for him. Witnessing his pain the other day hadn't been easy. Now it appeared a heavy weight had lifted off him and the family.

Roland smiled at Jeanne. He held up a folder and waved it back and forth. "I brought sheet music and the Wednesday night lesson we discussed the other day. I meant to call you this morning, but Winston left a message with Sister Cheryl, and I hurried right over. I'm sorry. Will you forgive me? Are you still game to help me?"

An inward smile filled her, driving away the miserable doubt for good. "Yes. You're forgiven, and I can't wait to get started. We can work in the living room. How about we run the lesson by Renee's children later? Is that all right?"

Roland's eyes widened. "Wow. I forgot all about the little ones. Where are they?" He tilted his head and glanced down the hall.

Renee giggled. "In the backyard playing. Lunch is coming up in a few minutes, so they'll be in shortly. Did you want to stay? It'd be great to have a family meal again."

"Of course. I'd love to."

Jeanne stood and placed her glass in the sink. "I plan on treating them to ice cream after lunch at the shop on the square. Roland, will you help me wrangle the kiddos? Otherwise, they'll get a sugar high for sure."

Renee waggled a finger at Jeanne. "Not too much sugar. They won't sleep tonight."

Roland smiled and refilled his cup. "Don't worry, sis. We can visit the park afterward. I'm sure they'll burn off all their energy before getting home. Is that okay with you, Jeanne?"

"Sure." Jeanne cupped her cheek. "Oh. I can't go to the park. I promised to help Renee do the laundry. Another time would be great."

"We can always wash tomorrow. It's not going anywhere." Renee peeked at the full baskets beside the washer. "I can get a couple of loads done while you and the kids are gone."

Roland rose and stood between Winston and Renee. "Since we're all together, I've got some wonderful news. Well, I hope you'll think it is, and I wanted to tell you guys before someone beat me to it—Pastor Eli or Sister Cheryl, for instance." He grinned and then beckoned Jeanne closer. "You too, come on over. Eli and I met this morning. He offered me the youth minister position. I'd already prayed about the responsibility it'd entail, so I went ahead and accepted it. The job has a part-time salary. The pastor wants me to stay in his extra guest room until I get enough money to find my own place. I have already put my resumé in several places around town. Hopefully, soon, I'll be working two part-time jobs."

He placed a hand on his brother's shoulder. "Winston, I want you and Renee to know how much I appreciate your generosity and love, but I can't come back to the house to live. Too many memories, some bad but mostly good ones. I must move forward on the path God has set my feet on. Please, don't be angry."

Winston stood. "You're welcome here anytime. This old house has plenty of room for all of us if you change your mind…we're family. I understand completely, and I'm not mad."

"Thanks, brother. You have a family to raise, and this house will be a great place to do it in. One day I'll have a place of my own. Three." His smile widened, and he met Jeanne's gaze.

Winston's brow crinkled. "Three what?"

"Three kiddos, two boys and a girl."

Jeanne's heartbeat stilled in her chest. *Is this the man God has blessed me with? Oh, are You showing me the new direction in my life that You whispered to me? You have shown such grace to both Roland and me. I read the Isaiah forty-three passage, and it gave me much hope for my future.*

She gave a sharp head nod. "Roland, let's go to the living room to review the lesson and hymns. We only have a short time to coordinate. Let's make the most of it."

He grabbed the folder and followed. In the living room, he spread the contents on the coffee table. They sat, and he handed her the itinerary but quickly snatched it back. "Jeanne, we've only known each other a short while."

"Y-yeah." A breathy reply floated on the room's silence. Jeanne never wanted Roland's gorgeous blue-violet eyes to look away.

"To be honest, I'd like to get to know you better, and I'd sure like it if you didn't leave Grove Hill and return to Hopewell. Would you consider making this small town your home? I know this is fast, but when I saw you that day at the center, you captured my heart, and I've been falling for you ever since. I love you, Jeanne Adams." Roland glanced at his hands. “All I have to offer is my heart and these hard-working hands.” He turned over his palms toward her. “One day, that’ll all change. But right now, because of how I have lived the last few years, I feel unworthy to even speak to you, much less share my feelings.”

Jeanne slid her hands into his calloused ones. “Oh, Roland, you have plenty to offer. Jesus is in your heart foremost, I’ve seen that since we met, and I’ll always be happy to be second to Him in your life. You also captured my heart that day at the center—even though you were a bit grungy.”

Roland laughed.

Jeanne’s cheeks blushed, but she continued. “I love you too. Your sweet words of affirmation have aided in my future decision. I’ve prayed about this, and now I know His answer. I’m leaving next Thursday and will be gone for about a week, no longer than two. Renee and Winston have offered to let me live here, and they will talk to my father.” She flashed a tender but teasing grin. “I might be too independent to suit you. We briefly touched on the subject the other day before Sister Cheryl returned, but I’d like to attend college and much, much more. Also…three.” She waited for his response, expecting an honest but favorable reply of his steadfast love and the assurance of God’s path.

“No, you’re not at all too independent. I remember that you wanted to work with teen girls.”

"I haven't told Renee or any of my family any of this. Working as a sitter each week in the church nursery isn't what I want. Don't get me wrong, I'd count it a blessing to work in the nursery. My greatest joy would be to lead these young people to the Lord and help the girls with their daily issues. We get off track and need a little nudge back onto the rails. I know it's a big aspiration, but I want to be a licensed counselor or therapist for teen girls."

"This is great." His eyes shone like bright blue stars. "We can work as a team, me with the boys, girls for you to start with, but eventually, I feel my purpose is to be a clergyman. We can attend college together and see if our next steps lead us to seminary. Whatever we decide on, we'll do it as a couple." He paused, drew a breath, then tilted his head and hiked one dark eyebrow. "So…what did you mean by what you said…three?" He gently settled his hand on hers.

"Two boys and a girl." She giggled, and heat rose in her cheeks.

Roland lifted her hand while he held her gaze. Then he gently pressed the back of her hand against her lips and leaned in to kiss the palm. "Thank You, Lord," he whispered.

A small breath escaped from Jeanne's lips. She gently moved her hand away from her mouth but knew she would never forget that first oddly moving kiss…her hand against her lips, his lips against her hand. Even at the memory, her palm tingled. "Roland, I have so much to tell you. But I'd like to talk later at the park while the kids play."

"Sure." His smile ignited all the dark, numb places in her heart. "Let's go over the lesson."

Jeanne lifted a silent, thankful prayer heavenward. *In Your infinite wisdom, You have brought me to Roland and him to me. We never knew what awaited us at the doorsteps of Your grace, but I'm so glad for the love You have bestowed upon our hearts. No matter what happens, we can be sure that our destiny is in Your hands. Thank You, Jesus. Amen.*

Joy bubbled in her soul as she sat close beside the man whom God had selected to be her companion in life. She met his gaze with a warm smile and found him waiting for her.

Her first. Her last. Her forever.

Love Echoes

Aurora Hearts series, book 1

Excerpt

"We must have a new baby calf. I heard the mother celebrate its arrival around 2 o'clock this morning." Maggie Lynn Rivers' footsteps quickened toward the calving pens eager to witness yet another of God's gifts. Her inherited ranch sprawled across three-thousand acres in Utica, Texas.

Spring yearned to be let loose, but winter refused to abandon its hold. Orange and pink icy puddles glinted across the barnyard as the sunrise inched upward. Frost-covered leaves on a small patch of Hosta's were ready to bloom in the barn's shade.

Her boots sunk deeper in the mud with each step toward the corrals. Last night's rain was heavier than usual for this time of spring. *Oh man, I forgot my muck boots.* She heaved a heavy sigh, refusing to let anything deter her mission, regardless of the terrains sloppiness.

Wide-eyed, Maggie halted dead in her tracks. A sharp pain ripped through her gut as her gaze fell at the base of the old timber barn, a figure of a large dog lay mangled. Blood matted and stained the once soft tri-color Australian Shepard coat—her dad's beloved dog, Blue…dead. She rushed toward him, stopped at his side, and dropped to her knees.

Maggie had stroked his shiny fur the prior evening, now the luster was gone. Tears streamed off her chill-bitten rosy cheeks. Flesh torn from his throat showed the final blow. She reached out to scratch behind his ear, then paused. The thought of touching Blue with gloves appeared somehow disrespectful. Peeling off her work gloves, she stroked the companion's ear as she always did. Numb, she shrugged off her blue-jean work jacket and blanketed his body. Sobs clogged her throat. "I, I'm sorry, Blue."

Beyond the barn upon the low hill something caught Maggie's attention, and she shielded the sting of the rising sun. The faint image became more prominent through her fingers. Standing against the orange, and pink sky, a lone white wolf, held his ground.

The cold dawn met with his billowing breath as it swirled from his nostrils. Intention to dominate and wreak fear aired when his muzzle lifted and released a low, throaty, blood-curdling howl. The stark shriek would've sent a lesser woman cowering, but not Maggie. He killed her friend. With a clenched fist, she stood to face the beast.

Red-devilish eyes pierced her soul. Again the creature emitted an unconstrained low growl. A set of bloodstained canines showed his victory. She glanced at Blue and then back at the animal. He had vanished.

A frigid wind swept from the family cemetery, cutting Maggie to the bone. The sweet fragrances of two blossoming wisteria bushes reminded her of a long-awaited promise she *mus*t keep. The mounting emotions took all of her courage on each step toward the toolshed.

Searching for the proper implements, Maggie bumped against the adjacent barn wall, startling the next-door occupants. Four whinnies and a few snorts sounded their displeasure.

An empty wooden box sat on a high shelf, higher than her five-foot-two stature. She jumped. Her fingertips caught the box's edge, and it landed at her feet. Then a dusty cloud rained over her cowgirl straw hat. "This should be the right size."

She pulled a rawhide strap off a rusty nail, tied back her long strands, plucked a shovel off the rack, and grabbed the box.

Spears shot through her heart when she stopped at the base of the sparse gravel path. *Courage, Maggie Lynn.*

Lifting her shoulders, she took one step and then another, pulling the heavy spade behind. The clanks resounding on the rocky path didn't help.

When I was sick from the accident with Anna, you never left my side, dear Blue. Cal tried to feed you, but you never ate until I did. You were the only friend I could count on when mom died. Those blue eyes sparkled every time your head rested in my lap. I'll miss you, old pal.

The family cemetery was as old as the ranch itself, almost. William and Katie McNeil built the Aurora in 1825 and passed along the property, always to a son, until Maggie's birth. Her father insisted everyone call her 'Miss Maggie.'

Her muddy boot kicked open the wrought-iron gate. A squeak shrilled, then the metal clattered against the fence, sending chills along Emma's spine. Locating the promised plot, she drove the spade into the ground. The earth didn't give way, and for a good reason—it was half-frozen and a bit rocky. Persistence took over her grief, and an hour later, the final shovel of soil was heaped on top of the rest. She swept away tears with her sleeve. Her gaze lifted to the cloudless sapphire sky and swallowed to halt further flows.

On her trek back to Blue's body, four dark silhouettes overhead circled the barn. "No, no, no!" She screamed. To protect her friend, she took off in a run, shooing away the predators, and then a jolt of air escaped when she landed at his side. She peeled back the jacket and was relieved to see his body still intact. She gently stroked behind his ear, the warmth he once possessed gone, now he was cold and stiff.

Maggie gathered Blue in her arms. Shaky legs rose, and halfway up, she dropped onto the ground. Sucking in a breath and collecting what little strength left, she tried again. But this time, she crashed on top of Blue. "I won't and can't be defeated. Dad, I promised you, and I'll keep it. Lord, help me." Sliding the jacket off Blue, she gripped a front and a back leg and tugged. He didn't budge, so she lifted her gaze to heaven.

She drew a gaunt breath and tugged until his body slid onto the jacket. "Thank you, Lord." Another firm grip on the sleeves, she dragged Blue's body up the hill.

Winded when she reached the top, she doubled over. Sweat dripped from her forehead and onto the empty box. She straightened and stared at her dad's headstone. His deep voice chimed in. *Promise me. You'll bury Blue next to me when the time comes.*

"I love you, Dad."

Maggie continued with the unplanned burial. Turning the container on its side, she rolled Blue in. Cloaking his body with the muddy, bloodstained jacket, she stared into his gentle face. With one final stroke behind his ear, she closed the lid and inched the box into the hole. A tear splattered on each shovel of soil heaved on top. Finished, she tamped the mound one final time.

Two wisteria bushes twined behind her parent's headstones, full of lavender buds many ready to burst open any day. This lovely display is forever etched in her memory. "Dad, you planted the first bush behind Mom's gravestone eight years ago. You spent hours talking to Mom and even insisted she appeared to you in a fog. I planted the second bush when you left for your final home five years ago. Each spring, the shrubs grow fuller and more beautiful together, just like your love for one another. I'm sorry that I didn't take better care of Blue."

Branches rattled overhead. A cold chill rushed through Maggie. She withdrew the rawhide strap from her hair and gathered two fallen limbs to fashion a makeshift cross. With the back of the shovel, she whacked the top of the vertical branch into the ground until it was seated. "There. That'll have to do until I get you a proper headstone."

Pulling off her straw hat, her soiled and bloodstained hands clasped the crown and held it against her chest. "Dad, Blue is with you and Mom. Blue, you'll have a wonderful time chasing all the balls dad tosses. I know you'll fish and hunt like always. Take care of each other. I love you all very much."

Maggie stepped over to little Anna's grave and drew a breath. "I wished you could've known Blue. He saved me that day, but I couldn't save you, baby girl. If only— Rusty bolted, my boot tangled in the stirrup, and I was dragged. God led Blue to find Sam. Anna, I was devastated, and now I'm unable to have another baby. I ought not to have been on that horse. I'm sorry, baby."

For twenty-two years, Maggie'd never imagined leaving the ranch regardless of any challenges. From the plateau, her gaze washed over the land. It never failed to awe her with the breathtaking view of the valley, meadows, and woods that confined the ranch's acreage. Above, songbirds sang sweet melodies, and just below, brooks meandered through lush pastures where wildlife watered.

Maggie's back stiffened at the sound of a shotgun chambering a shell. She turned just when Cal, her husband of four years, was taking a bead on a clump of bushes just beyond the cemetery's wrought-iron fence.

Cal's life on the rodeo circuit ended the same year they married. His tall physique, jet-black hair, and brown eyes captured her heart when Matt Daniels, a neighbor, and a friend, introduced them.

He lowered the weapon and gave a sharp nod at the freshly turned earth. "Is that Blue you buried?"

"It is." She whispered.

"Was it the wolf?"

Sobs clogged her throat. "Yes."

Anger flashed in Cal's eyes. "This has to stop here and now. I've had enough of that wolf hunting our stock. The creature only kills for pleasure. Sam saddled two horses for us to corral the yearlings and vaccinate, but instead, we'll hunt down that demon."

Sam Miles had been Aurora's foreman for nine years. His handsome features fit his rugged six-foot-tall, with sandy hair and brown eyes. Alcoholism nearly destroyed his career, and for a good reason—an accident—he was heartbroken over his wife and child's death.

Maggie closed the space between them. Anger shrouded his face. She hadn't seen this expression from her husband. He never let rage overtake his gentle persona. "We can't afford to lose any more of the herd. I was on my way to the calving pen when I found Blue. I'll check the pens before riding out to mend the fences."

Cal pulled her tight under his muscular arm. "I'm sorry about Blue. I would've buried him if you asked." His finger twined and smoothed an unruly tress that had fallen across her forehead. "You have a right to cry, but I prefer to see those lovely green eyes, not bloodshot. Dry those tears. I can't stand to see you in so much pain."

Maggie swallowed back the sobs and nodded. "I'll try. I had to bury him myself, I promised Dad. Do me at least one favor, and get that killer."

"I will." His lips brushed against her forehead and lingered for a kiss.

She leaned into his body. "This time, that wolf didn't kill some calf or a chicken—it was a friend."

"Joe and Bob drove out to the west pasture to feed the herd. Sam and I'll do a quick sweep of the ranch and be back by dinnertime. When you're alone, carry a rifle more now than ever since he's killed this close to the house. It won't be forever just until we catch this beast."

The Snyder men, brothers from Oklahoma, had started at the ranch two years earlier after their mother passed away from cancer. The men's loyalty surpasses their goofiness as they stumble over each other. Once, they shared a picture of their mother with Maggie. Both took after her features and stature, five feet six, and the young men often showed how big their hearts are with those they care about.

"Cal, we've talked this over before, and you know how I feel about guns."

"I don't want you caught off guard if this beast shows up while you're alone or unprotected. You know how easy Rusty spooks."

Maggie eased out of his arms. "Don't go there about Rusty. I'll think about the gun. Anything else happening around the ranch?"

"Nothing much to mention. I left you three carrots on your grandpa's bench. See you later, sweetheart." He turned, swung the gun's muzzle around, rested the stock on his shoulder, and headed down the hill.

Nothing to mention—what do you mean? You take on stuff you shouldn't and treat me like this isn't my ranch.

Maggie jerked a red bandanna from her snug back pocket and wiped her face and bloodstained hands. She headed toward the pens hoping it would lift her spirits with the sight of the mother and new baby.

Spring brought with it peak calving season, giving the cattle ranch a good start such as the Aurora, and this year was no exception. Maggie never imagined her ranch to run cattle, but it did. When her father passed, so did his wealthy knowledge of horse breeding. Strained finances didn't let her continue the tradition at the time. Her dream would have to wait.

Over forty calves were born since the beginning of the year. Cal herded the heifers into the pens two weeks before their babies were due to drop.

Halfway down the hill, Maggie heard a bawling heifer. She rushed to the corral and skidded to a stop on the slick mud. A distraught mother stood over her newborn calf. Blood pooled around the mangled, lifeless, black Angus baby. Caught on the railing was a tuft of white fur. She dislodged the pelt and slid the remnant into her pocket. This scrap gave her proof of what killed the baby. *The white wolf.*

She hoisted herself upon the second rail to survey the corral for other ill-fated deaths—relieved to find none. One leg swung over the top, then she landed on the other side flat-footed in a sloppy puddle.

After a lifetime of working on a ranch, Maggie knew the mother would protect her young and could charge at any moment, even if the baby was dead. She tromped through the muck to open the adjacent pen gate. She waved her arms, trying to separate the two, but the mother didn't budge. *I need a prod to get you moving. Where did I leave that noisy thing yesterday?* She disliked using harsh devices, but it was the only way.

Maggie spotted the contraption hanging on the outer barn wall. She climbed over the pipe fence, retrieved the device, and rushed back. The mere sound prompted the mother to step away with reluctance, but she continued to voice her displeasure at leaving her baby.

With the mother secured in the enclosure, she hurried to get the tractor. Again, she hoisted herself over the fence. Her muddy boot slipped and caught between the rails. Suddenly, she landed in a precarious position, upside down with the ends of her hair dangling in a puddle.

The awkward predicament allowed a chuckle to escape past her pent-up heartache. She twisted her foot, freeing her boot. Upright, the wet ends of her hair slapped against her face, and a speck landed in one eye. Blindly, her hand searched for her bandanna and wiped the debris out. *I'm glad it wasn't blood.* She removed the slop from her hair and continued to the tractor.

A turn of the key and the engine gave a flat grinding sound. Maggie sighed and gave a swift kick to the side of the compartment, leaving her boot print. Again, she turned the ignition. This time, it roared. She shifted the gear into drive and took off with the tires, spinning a trail of mud behind the tractor.

Soft slush made steering tricky. The tractor slid to one side. Maggie turned the wheel, accelerated the gas, and maneuvered back into a straight line. She skidded to a stop at the corral, set the brake, and then jumped off into another puddle. *Let this serve as my lesson, never to forget my muck boots.*

Maggie slapped her gloves together to knock off the embedded sludge and slipped them on. She gripped the calf's foot and dragged her underneath the bottom railing. With one final push, the body slid into the bucket and laid the bloody gloves beside the calf. To relieve the mother, she took the baby out of sight to the backside of the barn and switched off the tractor's engine.

Maggie rounded the barn corner as Joe pulled in and parked the ranch truck. "Morning, Miss Maggie. What's up?" His short stature exited the vehicle, then he ran a hand through his sandy hair and planted a dirty ball cap on top.

"We had a newborn calf down in the pen. The poor thing is in the tractor bucket behind the barn. We need to bury her."

"I'll do it, Miss Maggie. Don't you worry yourself. Was it that wolf again?"

"Yes." She swallowed. Her reply drove a spike into her heart.

Joe scanned the area. "Where's Blue? I haven't seen him. He usually rides with me to feed the herd."

She bit back tears, and then her voice hardened. "That wolf killed him last night. I buried him next to my dad."

"I'm sorry—"

A howl echoed from the hill next to the graveyard. They froze and looked toward the knoll.

"Joe, do you have your gun?"

His gaze shot toward the truck. "No, ma'am, I don't."

Maggie pulled out the hidden tuft of white fur and raised it for comparison. Another blood-curdling howl filled the air. After a final lunge, the wolf ran into the woods.

~ About the Author ~

Elle H. Raye writes God's message with inspirational tales in an array of romantic dips and bends. Small-town living flourishes in her novels, novellas, and short stories. The author makes her home in the deep Piney woods of East Texas with her Boxer, Honey, whose favorite pastime is playing squirrel tag.

Visit Elle's website for updated book releases. www.ellehraye.com

~ Other Titles by Elle ~

Aurora Hearts series

Love Echoes, book 1

Love's Destiny, book 2

Whispering Willow series

Willow Tree Hearts, book 1

Stand Alone

Silent Memories

Summer's Whisper

Moonlight Dance

Honored Wish/short story eReader only

Shadows in Emma's Heart

Ingram Content Group UK Ltd.
Milton Keynes UK
UKHW020804190723
425424UK00017B/284

9 798223 946168